Praise for Kate Perry's Novels

"Perry's storytelling skills just keep getting better and better!"

—Romantic Times Book Reviews

"Can't wait for the next in this series...simply great reading. Another winner by this amazing author."

—Romance Reviews Magazine

"Exciting and simply terrific."

—Romancereviews.com

"Kate Perry is on my auto buy list."

—Night Owl Romance

"A winning and entertaining combination of humor and pathos."

—Booklist

Other Titles by Kate Perry

The Laurel Heights Series:

Perfect for You

Close to You

Return to You

Looking for You

Dream of You

Sweet on You

Tamed by You

Here With You

The Family and Love Series:

Project Date

Playing Doctor

Playing for Keeps

Project Daddy

The Guardians of Destiny Series:

Marked by Passion

Chosen by Desire

Tempted by Fate

Here With You

Kate Perry

Phoenix Rising Enterprise, Inc.

For you.

Thank you for aiding and abetting me. Without your cheers and encouragement, I'd be... Well, truthfully, I'd probably be an international jewel thief. Or the bodyguard for a major movie star. Or (most likely) huddled in a dark corner, rocking back and forth.

Anyway, this book is for you.

I wish you friendship, success, and love—everything the women of Laurel Heights enjoy.

And also...

Kisses to my Magic Man. No woman could ask for a better hero.

Also, I may have used a couple lines from your wedding vows in this book. What can I say—you inspire me.

Chapter One

NORMALLY WHEN NICOLE, Marley, and Valentine went to Grounds for Thought, they sat at the round table in the window and drank coffee. But this wasn't a normal evening. Tonight, Nicole sat on the counter and swung her feet while she drank champagne.

Tonight was Valentine's wedding reception.

Nicole surveyed the scene with her expert eye. Everything was perfect, from Valentine's dress to the way they looked at each other. Joyous. The bride glowed and the groom looked besotted. At least that was the way his expression would have been described in the historical romances Nicole loved to read.

Romantic.

She sighed. She loved romance.

When she was a little girl, she demanded that

her parents read her the stories where the prince swept the girl off her feet. She loved pink and roses and chocolate.

As an adult, her tastes had refined. Instead of roses, she preferred tulips. Red was her color now, and chocolate...

Well, she still loved chocolate.

She'd also found a passion for lingerie. So much so that she'd quit her job as an office manager and gone to work at Romantic Notions in Laurel Heights. She'd been there for over half a year, and she was still going strong. She'd never stayed at any job for that long.

She loved her job. She sold more than expensive scraps of lace and silk—she sold romance. She helped women turn dreams into reality.

She sold Happily Ever After.

Everyone deserved Happily Ever After.

She looked forward to her own. She didn't doubt that she'd get one, she just didn't know what it'd look like. Or who would be involved. She'd just broken up with her boyfriend—not that it was a loss. Sure, she was sad, but he hadn't been right for her in the long run.

Finding the right person was key. Marriage was forever. She understood the logical arguments: people changed and you couldn't predict if you'd be with someone for all your lives.

Whatever.

She didn't buy those arguments. If you loved someone enough to marry him, you worked at it and fixed your problems—you didn't bale at adversity. Marriage was sacred. Her mom and dad were testament to it. Valentine and Ethan, too.

One day, she vowed, as she watched all the love and happiness before her.

One day she'd find the right person. Someone who was on her side and encouraged her to be more. Someone who'd have her back no matter what. A best friend who excited her mentally and physically.

She'd had a best friend once who'd been like that. They'd only been friends, but she'd often wondered if they couldn't be more one day.

Until he'd left to pursue becoming a musician and never talked to her again.

Not that she wanted to think about Griffin Chase. Today was a day of happiness, and remembering Grif never made her happy.

"You look sad," the man standing next to her said. "Or like you're gonna punch someone out."

She looked at Bull. She'd just met him that evening; he was a good friend of Valentine's new husband. He was a mountain of a man with muscles on top of muscles, a bald head, a UV tattoo of a dandelion along the side of his face, and a heart of gold. Nicole had liked him instantly. They'd only known each other for, literally, minutes, and he already felt like a brother.

"I'd rather dance." Smiling, she hopped off the counter. "Want to?"

"Let's get down." He set his drink aside and held out his hand. "But don't get ideas about me. You're cute and all, but I'm not your type."

"You know my type?" she asked with a grin as he led her to the dance area.

"Yeah. Younger and prettier than me." He nodded to the front door. "Like that dude who just walked in."

She looked at who he pointed out, and then she tripped. He was wearing a cowboy hat low on his forehead and sunglasses despite the late hour, but she recognized him despite the disguise.

Based on the way the party around them quieted, other people did, too. Not surprising—his music had blown up. Griffin Chase was a household name and had a face everyone knew. He'd always wanted to hit it big. She wasn't surprised at how successful he'd become. His music was emotion transformed into sound, unique and all his own even in its widespread appeal. Add his voice to the mix and he was destined to be a star.

"You okay?" Bull steadied her. "I know I have two left feet, but even I've never knocked over a girl before I started dancing with her."

"No, I'm fine," she said, watching her former best friend, who'd been M.I.A. for nearly a decade, zero in on her. He sauntered with deceptive laziness. There'd never been anything lazy about him—he always had a purpose. She just wondered why that purpose brought him here.

Bull scowled. "You know that dude?"

"I used to." At one time she knew him better than anyone. They used to hang out in her backyard, sharing their hopes and dreams, talking about all the places they were going to go one day. Places he'd gone without her.

Griffin Chase stopped in front of her and took his sunglasses off. The stormy gray eyes that women all over the world swooned over were aimed right at her. "Hello, Nicole."

Nicole stood face-to-face with the man she thought she'd never see again. He looked familiar and like a stranger all at once, like the urban cowboy the media labeled him: jeans, boots, and an untucked shirt under a dark jacket. A leather necklace disappeared into the vee of his collar.

His face was harder, the soft edges of adolescence gone. His stance was casual, with his hands in his pockets, but he vibrated with energy. Grif looked both like the boy she'd known and the rock star she occasionally saw on magazine covers in the grocery store.

He looked hot, actually. He'd always been attractive, but now there was an intensity about him that made you think about sweaty nights and tangled sheets.

Bull shifted next to her. "Hey, you're—"

"Bull, this is Griffin Chase." She pressed herself against her new friend's arm, mostly for support, but she didn't mind the frown it caused Grif.

"I'll be damned." A wide smile split Bull's face. "I loved your last album, man. I worked out to it every day for a couple months."

Grif shook the man's outstretched hand. "You're Kelly Torres, right? I saw you fight in Vegas last year."

"Which match?"

"Against the Cheetah."

"That wasn't a match, that was a mauling. Cheetah didn't stand a chance against me," Bull said modestly. "I've got one coming up with Georgie Boy Rocklin this summer. That's a worthy one to see. Let me know. I can hook you up."

Nicole rolled her eyes. "Sorry for breaking up the mutual admiration society, but what are you doing here, Grif?"

He returned his gaze to hers. "I need to talk to you."

"Now?" She looked around at the celebration happening. More than a few people were staring at them and whispering.

He looked around, too. "I'm sorry my timing isn't great, but we both know it'd have been awkward regardless."

An understatement. She hadn't seen him since right after high school ended. "Because it's been nine years."

He had the grace to wince. "I know and it's completely my fault. You're entitled to rant at me, if you want."

Sighing, she shook her head. "I don't want to rant at you. I just don't understand why you're here."

"You kiddies should take this private." Bull kissed her cheek and patted her butt. "Play nice with him, or he'll immortalize you as a witch in his next song."

"Thanks for the warning." She patted his butt in return. "Rain-check on the dance?"

"You betchya." He winked at her and rejoined the crowd.

Nicole faced Grif, her stomach jittery. The way he watched her was unnerving. It wasn't her best friend's gaze — it was the direct stare of a man who wanted something from her.

Not that they'd ever been like *that*. Why her mind was going there, she had no idea.

"Shall we?" He motioned to the door.

Nicole led the way, brushing by him quickly, aware of the muffled thud of his boots following close behind. She stepped into the doorway to the left, away from any prying eyes in Grounds for Thought, and faced her past.

"This is weird." She wrapped her arms around herself, to protect herself from Grif as much as the evening wind. The flirty dress that had seemed perfect for the wedding didn't offer any protection from the chill air.

He took his jacket off and offered it her. "I'd been meaning to come see you for a while, actually."

She stared at the beat-up leather.

When she didn't make a move to take it, he draped it around her shoulders. It was warm from his body and somehow more intimate than it should have been. It smelled spicy, nothing like the sun-scented boy who'd been her friend.

Grif leaned against the stucco wall, the intensity of his gaze belying his laid-back posture. "The timing never seemed right. So much time passed, and I knew I didn't deserve your friendship, much less have the right to intrude on your life."

"But you're here now," she pointed out.

He exhaled deeply. "I need your help."

She nodded. He'd said as much earlier. It made sense that he'd come back because he needed something from her, but it didn't hurt any less. "I'm not sure what I can help you with. Don't you have a team of people who help you with things?"

"Yes, but only you have what I need."

How many times had she laid in bed at night and wished for a man to say that to her, just like that, with a voice full of dark desire?

But it was Grif. How much could he really want her, if he couldn't bring himself to even call her once in all this time? "How would you know? You haven't seen me in years."

"My family gives me updates." He smiled apologetically. "My parents still live next door to yours. You know how your mom and dad love to rave about you."

They did. Usually she thought it was so cute, but in this case she wished they'd kept their mouths shut.

"It's cute," Grif said, as if reading her mind. "But they've always adored you."

She curled into herself, confused—not sure

what to think or feel. "Not that this catching up isn't nice, but I'm still wondering why you're here."

"I want to live with you."

Her mouth fell open. *"Excuse me?"*

"Just for a couple weeks."

"A couple weeks?" She goggled at him, waiting for him to say he was just kidding. But he stood there calmly watching her. She shook her head. "Is someone feeding you crack?"

"I know I have no right to ask this, but I need a quiet place to work on my next album. I have some songs done, but I don't have a solid piece to anchor the whole thing together."

"Don't you rock stars have a place you go to work in peace? Some island in the Caribbean or something?"

"Yes, but I need you."

Every night, millions of women dreamt of Griffin Chase standing before them, looking them in the eye, and saying he needed them. Probably tens of millions.

But not her. She folded her arms across her body. "Kind of like you've needed me all these years?"

"I deserve that." He nodded.

"Oh, you deserve *way* more than that." She glared at him. "You *left* me. We had all sorts of plans to travel together, and you left. I understand you were pursuing your dreams, but you could have sent an email every now and then. Or, heck, even a text."

"I know—"

"You don't know." She knocked his shoulder with her hand. "You were my best friend. We were together every day for years, and then you disappeared. How is that cool?"

"It's not." He took her hand and secured it against his heart.

She refused to be distracted—or excited by his touch. He was just holding her hand, she told herself. He didn't have his hand down her pants.

Which was *not* something she was going to think about.

He moved closer, so she felt the force of his gray eyes. "I was a selfish jerk, Nicole."

She motioned with her free hand, "More."

"A complete dog."

"Try harder."

His brow furrowed in thought. "Brown, foamy pond scum?"

She shrugged. "That's closer, I guess."

"The worse part is that I knew what a mistake I was making." He rubbed her palm with his thumb. "I missed you, Nicole. I just got caught up in work."

"You aren't helping your case." Bothered by his touch in a way that confused her, she retracted her hand but immediately regretted it.

"I lost sense of everything that was grounding in my life," he said quietly, ignoring her sarcasm.

"And now you want to be grounded again."

"No, I want to remember why I loved music so much." He looked away. "I've been thinking about quitting."

"*What*? Music has always been your life. Always."

"It's not making me happy anymore."

Of all the things she'd expect to come out of his mouth, those words weren't even on the list.

But it was something she understood. How many jobs had she started because she thought they'd been perfect only to find out they weren't what she wanted either? Too many to count. "Then change what you do," she suggested.

He shook his head. "I'm not like you."

The way he said it didn't sound like a compliment. "What does that mean?"

"Well, you've always jumped from one thing to the next."

"You say that like it's bad. I like to try new things." Her parents always told her she was smart and talented—she'd find her calling. She impatiently wondered when, but she didn't need someone like Grif pointing out her deficiencies. "Why do you have to write another album? I assume you have enough money to live on an island, drinking from coconuts, for the rest of your life."

"I can't just quit. People count on me. I employ people, and if I don't produce they're out of a job and paycheck."

"You can't be responsible for the world."

"I'm not responsible for the world. I'm just responsible for my corner of it. I'm responsible for my manager, who spends a fortune each month to ensure that his special needs daughter has every tool available to learn and grow. I'm responsible for the musicians who play with me, who work hard to scrape together a living for families while still being true to their calling. I'm responsible to every person who writes me, to thank me for helping them get through a difficult time in their lives with my music. This is beyond me, Nicole."

She gaped at him, shocked at the passion in his voice. In his eyes there was a maturity she'd never seen, and his words weighed heavily with sincerity.

When had she ever felt that sort of passion or drive? Never. Part of her felt bad for all the weight on his shoulders; part of her envied him. "Okay, I understand that you need help to revive your creative juices, but I don't understand why you have to live with me."

"Accessibility."

She didn't think she wanted to be *that* accessible to him.

"And I need to be away from questions and prying eyes. I need privacy to regain balance. I'm tired, Nic." Grif lifted the hat and ran a hand over his hair. "I need a quiet place away from all the noise my life generates. I need to remember why I loved music in the first place."

His frustration was written all over his face. He looked so lost, her heart broke for him. But how was she going to help him find the path back to his calling when she couldn't do that for herself? She'd been trying to find her own way—unsuccessfully—for so long.

Only he watched her with complete faith and trust that was both humbling and seductive. She liked the idea of being needed, especially by Griffin Chase.

It was a big responsibility. He wanted to *live* with her. She looked at how he'd filled out and grown up and knew having him crash at her apartment would be an experiment in masochism.

That was never happening.

Except she couldn't turn him away. It didn't matter that he'd been a jerk over the past few years. At one time she'd loved him more than anyone, and she couldn't turn her back on that.

She exhaled. "Okay, I'll help you."

He looked as shocked as she felt.

She cleared her throat. "So let's just get this straight. I help you rediscover your love for music—"

"And find inspiration for a title song for my album," he added.

"Okay." Piece of cake, right? "And then you'll go away again."

"Yes."

She didn't like that he agreed so quickly. It was inevitable, but he didn't have to sound so eager about it. "I have to check with my roommate, but it should be okay for you to crash on our couch for a few days. Come over tomorrow. But it's only temporary, and if Susan objects you're gone."

"You're an angel, Nic." He stepped forward and lowered his head to hers.

His mouth was on hers.

Grif was *kissing* her.

Her eyes wide open, she stared at him as his lips brushed gently over hers. Then she realized he watched her too, and she closed her eyes really quickly.

Which made the kiss worse, because it made her feel every slow, coaxing nibble.

It was delicious. It was everything a kiss should have been — warm, a little lip, a little tongue. Moist. Making her want more.

It freaked her out. She'd never felt anything like it, and she'd never expected to from Grif. He wasn't touching her and she could feel it all through her body.

When he finally ended the kiss, she wasn't sure whether to feel relieved or sad. Heart pounding, she tried to get herself under control. She bit her lip, trying to get rid of the imprint he'd left. She wanted to set her boundaries and tell him it wouldn't happen again, but she couldn't bring herself to say it.

Puzzled but not wanting to ponder it, she asked, "What was that?"

"We had to seal the deal," he said.

"A handshake is good for most people."

He put his sunglasses back on. "We aren't most people, Nic. See you tomorrow."

She watched him swagger away, his stride easy and loose, looking like a hero who'd ridden into town on a white steed.

But he wasn't a hero—certainly not hers.

She touched her lips, still feeling the sting of his kiss. What had she just got herself into?

Chapter Two

"I CAN'T BELIEVE you're leaving me. You just got here."

"Liar." Grif smiled at his friend KT as he stuffed a pair of jeans into his duffle bag. "You hate having people around. When I showed up on your doorstep, you barely resisted the urge to slam the door in my face."

"Well, I can't deny that. Especially when it's a man with a bag and his guitar." She lounged across her guest room's bed. KT lived like a hermit in the mother-in-law unit of her parents' palatial home. They'd met at a party years ago, after his first hit single *Lost*. KT had been hiding behind a huge potted plant, looking miserable, and they'd ended up in the music room with her critiquing *Lost*.

"Remember how you told me you never dated

musicians?" He yanked a shirt out from under her. "I'd like to point out that I ended up in your bed."

"My *guest* bed." She kicked him half-heartedly. "I still don't fraternize with musicians. They're all crazy."

"Yourself included?"

She held two fingers up. "I cannot tell a lie."

Grif smiled. KT was unique, with her own set of quirks, but she was the most talented songwriter he'd ever met. She only wrote for other people and never sang in front of anyone, but that first night they'd met she'd had one too many shots of whiskey and had broken her rule. Angels coveted her voice. He'd asked her once why she wouldn't sing more, but she'd told him to buzz off in less polite terms.

He looked around the room to make sure he remembered everything. His guitar, Tallulah, waited for him by the door. He hadn't opened her case since the last night of the tour he'd just ended. That was three months. He missed her, but at the same time he had no desire to touch her.

"There's this." KT held up his necklace.

"Thanks." He took the leather chain and slipped it over his head.

"How metrosexual of you." His friend smirked at him.

He didn't bother to reply. He wore it because it gave him a place to hang the arrowhead Nicole had given him before he'd set out to make a name for himself. As he'd packed up his car, she'd hugged him, slipped it into his hand, and whispered, "For protection, and to think of me."

KT stretched her long body, hugging a pillow to her. "So tell me about this woman you love."

"It's not like that," he said as he zipped up his bag and set it next to his guitar case. "We've been best friends since junior high."

"It's like that, especially if you're hiding out from your entourage to hang out with her on the sly."

"I told you why I'm hanging out with her."

"To reawaken your muse." She made crazy eyes at him. "Stay with me and I'll bitch-slap your muse awake."

"Thanks for the offer," he replied dryly.

"What are friends for?" She sat up, the pillow still in her lap. "Really. I want to know what the woman who brings the great Griffin Chase to his knees is like."

Nicole was stunning.

It'd hit him right in the middle of his chest when he saw her. Luminous, with her glowing skin and dark shiny hair that trailed over her creamy shoulders.

In retrospect, he guessed he assumed he'd find the same girl he'd left. Pretty and popular Nicole: the smart and funny girl with the ever-ready laugh. The girl everyone loved because she always made a person feel better than he really was.

She was still all that, but with an added layer of complexity.

She was sexy.

Last night she'd worn a flirty dress that left her shoulders bare and knee-high red boots that made him want to strip that dress off and see her in nothing but the footwear. Her voice was even different than it had been years before—deeper, nuanced, and mysterious.

But her eyes got him the most. Her eyes showed the way to heaven.

"Well?" KT prodded him.

It wasn't supposed to be this complicated. He shook his head. "There aren't words to describe her."

"You're such a goner."

"I'm telling you, it's not like that. Look at us. I've stayed friends only with you."

"That's because we're like siblings, and incest grosses both of us out." She gave him a knowing look. "Don't tell me you've never kissed Nicole."

"Kiss" didn't begin to describe it. It'd been more like a wake-up call. He started to get turned on just thinking about the softness of her lips on his. He hadn't meant to do it—it'd been a heat-of-the-moment sort of thing—and now he couldn't get it out of his head.

He wanted to do it again. He wanted to kiss more than just her lips.

"I rest my case," KT said smugly.

He raked a hand through his hair. "I couldn't help myself. I just leaned down and went for it. I'm surprised she didn't slap me, and I can't believe she didn't tell me to take a hike."

"She loves you, too."

"Nine years ago, I left her and never called. She should hate me."

KT shrugged. "Love is a strange emotion."

"Love is overstating it."

"There are all sorts of love. It morphs and changes." She got up and patted his shoulder. "I hope in this case it morphs into what you want."

That was the thing: he didn't know what that was. He'd come back because he had this damn album to write and he'd lost his motivation. He'd closed his last tour date with *Lost* and had thought of Nicole, like he always did when he played that song, since it was about her. He'd walked off the stage, almost oblivious to the applause as he remembered how excited he'd been to write music back when he'd known her.

Somewhere along the way he'd lost that excitement.

He wasn't used to not knowing what he wanted. He was tired. He'd been on autopilot and couldn't remember what passion felt like.

Nicole had always been passionate about everything she did: drawing, dancing, reading… even babysitting. Her focus changed like the wind, but then that was her charm. Her enthusiasm had been infectious. Around her, life had been bright and inspiring.

He missed her. Obstructing her from his life had been the biggest mistake he'd ever made.

It'd been a crazy idea to track her down and—basically—accost her, but he'd been desperate. He was lucky she'd agreed. He knew he didn't deserve it. He'd just have to make sure he was worthy of her friendship this time.

KT patted his shoulder again. "You better suck up to her big time. Take her flowers or something."

"You think flowers would help?"

"Hell if I know." She tossed the pillow aside. "My sister gets squeally when her beaus send her stuff like that. It's a woman thing, right?"

"Aren't you a woman?"

She recoiled as if he'd insulted her. "Please."

Laughing, he half hugged her. "Thanks for letting me crash in your sanctuary. Thanks for being my friend."

She snorted but hugged him back. "Don't think this gives you an open door back when Nicole kicks you out."

Nicole wouldn't kick him out. He was going to make sure of it, and he wasn't going to question why it seemed do-or-die.

He loaded his few belongings into his vintage

Chevy and then headed to the address Nicole had given him of the store where she worked. According to his GPS, it was a short trip. KT lived on the upper edge of the neighborhood.

Miraculously, he found a spot big enough to park his car. As he maneuvered into it, his phone rang with "Eye of the Tiger."

His manager's special ringtone. Grif knew exactly what Roddy would say. *Where are you? Don't you know you have to tell me how to locate you? Are you writing? When the hell are you coming back?* Roddy Gallagher was a shark, but he was predictable.

Grif silenced the phone and got out of the car. Later he'd talk to Roddy. Now he had to focus.

As he pulled up the address Nicole had texted him, he spotted a florist on the map.

He paused. Take KT's advice to heart? She wasn't a normal woman — she preferred spending time with her piano over any human, himself and her sister Bijou excepted. But she'd said Bijou loved flowers, and he couldn't think of a girlier girl than Bijou Taylor.

Flowers couldn't hurt. He headed to the shop, which was only a couple blocks away.

"Back to the Fuchsia," he read out loud as he approached. Cute. The door was open, and the space was inviting.

A thin brunette came out from behind a work-table as he walked in. "Can I help you?"

"I'd like"—he took off his sunglasses and surveyed all the colors, sizes, and shapes of flowers before pointing to pink ones in the corner—"those."

"Decisive."

"They look happy and cheerful." Just like Nic.

The woman plucked a bunch from the basket and inspected them. "You want anything else bundled in with the gerbera daisies? Some purple misties or miniature roses?"

"Just the pink flowers." Nicole was a simple woman. At least she used to be.

Not that it was apparent from the kiss last night. That kiss had been complicated. Hot. She'd been pliant and willing and warm in his arms. For *him*—he didn't have to question whether she kissed him for himself or because he was Griffin Chase, rock star.

In fact, she hadn't really wanted to kiss him.

Her body may have been willing, but he could tell her mind knew enough to hold back.

He wasn't sure how he felt about that.

Shaking his head, he brought himself back to the present.

The flower shop lady stood gawking at him. "You look just like Griffin Chase, but you couldn't be, because what are the chances?"

Damn—he should have worn the hat. He pulled out his wallet. "Pretty high, actually."

"You're saying you're the pop singer?"

He frowned. "I prefer calling my music crossover hits."

"Griffin Chase, who did *Lost*?"

"*Your laughter lights my way in the dark/Saving me, at any cost/From being lost,*" he sang. Those were his favorite lines. They reminded him most of Nicole.

The flower shop lady pointed at him, eyes narrowed. "You cannot hang out here. One celebrity is enough. And if you're high maintenance, you might as well buy your flowers somewhere else."

"I have no idea what you're talking about, but I have no intention of hanging out here. I just needed some flowers."

She didn't look like she believed him, but at least she wrapped up the flowers and carried them to the front counter.

"Those are pretty." He nodded at the bouquet as he handed money over. "She'll like them. Thank you."

The woman grunted and rang him up. "Thank me by buying more flowers."

"Okay."

She stopped what she was doing and gave him a disbelieving look.

"What's your name?" he asked, amused.

"Julie," she replied slowly.

"Julie, you're right. My friend deserves more than this. Can you send her a bunch of flowers every day?"

"Every day?" She goggled at him. "Her place will look like a funeral home. Unless she loves flowers?"

"I don't know." Nicole used to love fruit roll-ups and romance novels. He had no idea what she liked now. He'd have to find out. "Let's do every other day. If she hates it I'll cancel the order."

Julie handed over his change. "And I won't alert *The Enquirer* or anything."

"Deal. Send them to her work. You can charge my card." He gave her the information Nicole had given him. "Thank you, Julie."

She shook her head. As he walked out, he heard her mutter "Kooky celebrities."

Smart woman. Saluting her, he left the store and headed to Romantic Notions and Nicole.

Even if the name didn't give it away, he could tell from the storefront that it was over-the-top feminine. Fortunately, he'd never been the type of guy to shy away from women's underthings.

A soft bell chimed as he entered, the scent of vanilla tickling his senses. He stood in the doorway and looked around at all the lace and satin. Then he saw Nicole, standing next to a dresser, something frilly and red in her hand. She stared wide-eyed at him as though she hadn't expected to see him again.

Trying not to the think about her underwear and if she wore what she sold, he held out the bundle of flowers. "I got these for you."

Setting the lingerie down, she cautiously approached him. She accepted the pink bouquet, eyeing them like they might be poison. "What's the occasion?"

"Because you're being a good friend and I thought you'd like them." He frowned. "Do you like them?"

"They're beautiful," she said, looking confused. "I love flowers."

"I know you must get them all the time—"

"No." She shook her head.

"Your boyfriend doesn't give you flowers?" Not so subtle, but it'd been on his mind. His mom had told him Nicole was seeing someone. He told himself he was just curious, and that he didn't want his staying with her to cause friction.

Well, truthfully, he wanted her all to himself. It was selfish, but accurate.

Her brow furrowed. "My boyfriend and I broke up, but, no, he didn't give me flowers."

"He must have been an ass."

The corners of her mouth quirked. "Maybe."

He stuck his hands in his pockets. "I have my stuff in the car."

She set the lingerie down and held out a key. "My roommate has been out of town for work, but she comes back late tonight. I told her you're couch surfing for a few days, but if she can't take it, you're out."

"Got it." He took the keys.

"You can walk there. It's close." She bit her lip. "I have to work late, and then I have dinner with a friend, so you're on your own."

"Okay."

She looked like she was going to say something else, but then she just smiled gently. "We'll reawaken your passion for music, Grif. Trust me."

Oddly, he did. He already felt better than he had in months, maybe years.

Chapter Three

RACHEL SAT AT the back of her English class for two reasons. One: it was easier to zone out on the teacher. Two: back here no one could stare at her.

She was sick of being stared at.

In New York, no one had ever stared at her. She'd been the same as all the other students. They'd all worn uniforms, so she hadn't had to worry about figuring out what to wear, and she'd never stood out.

She'd done nothing but stand out since her dad had made her to come to San Francisco — and not in a good way.

She just wanted to go home. She wanted to go back to the apartment on the Upper East Side where she'd lived all her life. To the bedroom she hated because it was still decorated in princess pink from when she was a kid. She'd never complain about the pink ever again if her dad would just move them back.

But the apartment was gone. Sold. Her mom — also gone. Forever, because of a truck driver who hadn't had enough sleep.

Her nose prickled with tears. She rubbed the tip hard. Don't cry. Don't cry. *Don't cry.* As if they needed more reason to stare at her, especially Madison and Addison. They took great pleasure in making her feel as uncomfortable as possible.

It was her fault she was here, too. Part of her couldn't blame her dad for making them move. Getting drunk at that party had been dumb. Rachel hadn't even wanted to go, but she couldn't stand being at home alone, and she'd met that girl who'd seemed cool...

She wasn't sure how she'd ended up home. The last thing she remembered was this mod boy with severe acne pawing her until she finally locked herself in someone's bedroom. When she woke up, she was on the porch with her dad leaning over her.

And then she'd puked. A lot.

Her stomach revolted just thinking about it all. She was never touching alcohol ever again. Back in Manhattan, she knew kids who got trashed every weekend. Why would anyone do that to herself? She didn't get it.

Her dad had, of course, freaked out. According to her grief counselor, at sixteen getting drunk wasn't an "appropriate expression of her loneliness and sorrow."

The teacher paused in his lecture and glanced her way. Rachel sank in her seat and ducked her head. Hopefully he wouldn't call on her — she had no idea what he was talking about.

When she was sure the coast was clear, she pulled out her journal. It was reddish orange and gold, with a magnetic flap that closed to keep the pages from getting mangled.

As she opened it, a piece of paper slipped out and onto her desk. She didn't need to unfold the paper to know what it was: the poem she'd written for her mom right after her funeral.

Every line of it was written on her heart.

She hadn't written anything since.

After tucking the poem into her bag, she flipped to the very beginning of the journal, uncapped her favorite writing pen, and stared at the blank page.

She wasn't sure how long she sat there before she realized the other kids were shifting. Then the bell rang to signal the end of class.

The end of one torture, the start of another. She grimaced, thinking about going back to the huge house her dad had rented for them. It was ten times bigger than their apartment in Manhattan, and they were one person less. How did that make sense?

She packed slowly, waiting to leave after most of the class had filtered out. Slinging her bag across her body, she stood up and hurried to the door.

"Rachel. Can I see you a second?"

Sighing heavily, she turned around and walked back to her teacher. "Yes, Mr. Baker?"

"You can call me Michael, you know."

"Yes, Mr. Baker." In San Francisco, apparently the teachers liked to pretend they were your friends. And they dressed casually. If one of her teachers in New York had come to class wearing a tie-dye T-shirt and flip-flops like *Michael*, he'd be run out of town.

"Fine. Have it your way, Ms. Rosenbaum." He rolled his eyes. "I noticed you didn't turn in the letter I'd assigned yesterday."

Her turn to roll her eyes. They were reading *Pride and Prejudice*, so of course they had to write an old-fashioned letter. Typical. She'd read the book last year and they'd had the same assignment.

"I know you only transferred to Laurel Heights recently, but an assignment is an assignment." He raised his bushy eyebrows. "What's your excuse?"

"No excuse, Mr. Baker." *Just let me go.*

"Hmm." He stared at her, but she couldn't tell what he was thinking. Then he said, "Turn it in tomorrow, but you'll only get half credit."

"Thank you, Mr. Baker." She scurried out of the room before he could ask her anything else.

The good thing about having to talk to him was that the hallways were pretty cleared out. With any luck, her locker would be all clear, too.

But as she rounded the corner she deflated. No such luck. Madison and Addison were hanging out there—or the *⌐sons of anarchy*, as she liked to call them. Privately, of course.

Great. Just what she needed to cap her day. She hurried toward her locker, because based on her experience over the past few weeks, it was better to just get it over with, like ripping a Band-Aid off.

They began to snicker the moment they saw her. Lowering her head, Rachel fumbled as she opened her locker, her fingers clumsy.

Their snickering got louder.

She gritted her teeth and focused on the padlock. She should be used to their subtle ridicule after so many weeks. She should just ignore it. It didn't matter.

But it did.

Her lock clicked open and she exhaled in the small victory. She started to switch her books out, but one fell on the floor with a loud *bang*.

Rachel huffed, frustrated, bending over to pick it up.

Behind her, one of the girls—she couldn't tell if it was Madison or Addison—said, "I guess they wear white briefs in New York."

"At nursery school," the other one said dryly.

Hating herself for blushing, she stood and pulled her pants up as surreptitiously as she could. Her mom loved underwear and had drawers of it, in all sorts of colors. She'd made a big deal about taking Rachel on a big lingerie shopping expedition, but then she'd been killed, and updating underwear hadn't been a priority for Rachel. She had no idea how to buy underwear anyway, and there was no way she was going to ask her dad.

There was nothing wrong with her panties. They were white and simple. She wouldn't have even thought about it if she hadn't seen the colorful g-strings Madison and Addison wore.

"Rachel, haven't you graduated from nursery school yet?" Madison said with fake sweetness before they began laughing again.

She knew the tips of her ears were burning, but she focused on putting her things away so she could leave. As she zipped up the last book in her bag, she closed her locker and turned. Out of the corner of her eye, she saw the Griffin Chase poster Madison had taped in her locker.

Seeing it always made her crazy. Neither of the

—*sons of anarchy* deserved to listen to the genius of Griffin Chase. Griffin Chase understood sadness and loneliness in a way most people didn't. He understood love. He'd kept her company when her mom had just died, and still now when her dad worked all night and left her to roam the scary big house alone.

Her mom had been crazy for his music. When Rachel listened to his songs, she could almost hear her mom singing along.

Hiking her bag onto her shoulder, she shot Madison a glare, walked down the hall, and left the building.

She walked toward their house but she knew no one would be there. Her dad had been coming home from work really late. What was the point of going there?

Instead, she headed to the shopping area in the middle of Laurel Heights. She'd seen a lingerie shop there called Romantic Notions. Totally cheesy, but she had to start somewhere.

Rachel hovered outside the door. What size was she? What if her boobs were too small for a bra? How embarrassing would that be? She could already hear the *-sons* cackling at her lack of endowment.

What would she buy anyway? She had no clue.

If only her mom were here.

Ducking her head, she moved on before someone from school saw her lurking outside the shop. She went across the street, drawn by the Wi-Fi sign in the window of the coffee shop called Grounds for Thought.

She glanced in the window, wondering if she should enter. No classmates at least.

The blond woman at the counter looked up and waved her in.

Now she was going to look like a spaz if she didn't go in. Well, she wanted to check her email anyway. This was she could do it and still be around people, even if they were strangers. Someone was better than no one.

Sighing, she pushed open the door.

The aroma of coffee hit her as soon as she stepped inside. Just like her mom's office. She closed her eyes and breathed it in. She pictured playing on the floor between the reams of manuscripts while her mom sipped from her "Best Mom in the World" cup and edited one of her author's works. When she opened her eyes again, she almost expected to be transported back.

The blonde smiled. "It smells delicious in here, doesn't it? Are you looking for anything in particular?"

"Um, no." She checked out the glass case of pastries and pulled out her wallet. "Maybe just a hot chocolate and a Madeleine."

"Got it." After the quick transaction, the woman smiled again. "Want to sit down? I'll bring it over to you."

"Okay. Thank you." Rachel picked a table in the back corner and dragged her laptop out of her bag. While she waited for it to boot up, she flipped open her phone and checked for texts.

Nothing. She frowned at her cell. She'd only been gone a month but it was like her friends had forgotten her already. She couldn't remember the last time they'd texted.

"Nice," she muttered darkly. "Well, screw them."

She closed her phone and shoved it back in her bag's pouch. She glared at the pouch. If she let them go, she wouldn't have *anyone* left. So she took the phone back out, sent a quick text to her closest friend, Diana, and tucked it away again.

"Here you go, honey." The woman from the counter set a large cup topped with fluffy mounds of cream. "I hope you like whipped cream."

"I do. Thank you," she added politely.

The woman looked like she wanted to say something, but Rachel looked down and willed her to go.

It worked. She felt a shift of air as the woman went back to work. Rachel waited another minute to make sure and then opened her Gmail account.

No emails except for spam. Not shocking—her old friends always preferred texting. She liked email more. Texting was such an imprecise method of communication. Her mom and dad used to email her—all the time, even if they were in the other room and wanted her get ready for bed.

Rachel hit "Compose Mail" and began typing.

To: wendy.rosenbaum@gmail.com
From: rachel_rose@gmail.com
Subject: New School

Hi Mom.

I have this stupid homework assignment where I have to write a letter to someone. You're it.

Okay—it's not stupid. I know you're thinking how much I love writing letters. Remember when you helped me find that penpal in Switzerland when I was nine? I picked her because her name was Rachel too. She loved to ski, and her handwriting was as foreign as the way she wrote.

I'm at another new school. In San Francisco, but it might as well be Timbuktu. It was Dad's brilliant idea. I've been wondering if he's in league with Satan.

I hate it here. I hate this new school. I hate the people who giggle and run around like the world is perfect and sunny when it's dark and lonely and sad.

I hate that you won't be answering this email.

"Hey."

Rachel slammed the laptop shut, her head jerking up.

A boy stood over her. He was in a couple of her classes — she'd noticed him the first day, when he walked into English, surrounded by a bunch of his friends — so she guessed he was a sophomore too, even though he was so tall. His brown hair dipped into his blue eyes, and he pushed it back before sticking his hand in a jean pocket.

His mouth quirked. "Are you plotting some kind of crime? Going to rob this café of its croissants?"

She wanted to say something clever, something like what she'd write, but her tongue went all paralyzed in her mouth and it was all she could do just to mumble "No."

He stared at her, probably waiting for her to say more. When she didn't, he said, "I'm Aaron Hawke, and you're Rachel Rosenbaum."

"How —"

"I asked Michael, our English teacher." He smiled.

Her tongue twisted even more.

"Welcome to Laurel Heights High, Rachel Rosenbaum." He shifted his weight, and his hair flopped back onto his forehead. "See you tomorrow in class."

"Uh—I..." She watched him stop at the counter and chat with the blond woman before walking out.

Why had he come in here? She wanted to think he came in just to say hi to her—*he'd asked the teacher her name*—but she wasn't stupid enough to think she rated. He was probably just acting on a dare or something.

Without thinking, Rachel pulled out her reddish-orange notebook and a pen. She opened it and almost started writing. Habit. She couldn't remember ever *not* having a journal.

But she caught herself just in time. She set her pen down, torn between wanting to write and wanting to keep the journal fresh. Because this was the last journal her mom would ever give her.

Rachel pushed it aside, leaving it open to the first page. She picked up her hot chocolate and then set it down again, pushing it away, too. It was lukewarm now anyway, and the whipped cream had all melted away.

Chapter Four

NICOLE JERKED AWAKE as someone shook her shoulder. Gasping, she reached out in the dark.

Her roommate Susan fended off the weak attack and then turned on the bedside lamp. "Nicole," she whispered sharply. "I'm seeing things."

"What do you mean? What time is it?" Rubbing her eyes, she checked the time. "It's three-thirty in the morning, Susan!"

"No kidding. My flight was delayed, and then my bags were misplaced. I just got home. But forget that." She leaned down. "Either Griffin Chase is in our living room, or I'm having delusions brought on by fatigue and vodka."

"You're not having delusions. I told you I invited a friend to crash on the couch for a few days, remember?"

"*Griffin Chase* is your friend?" Susan exclaimed.

"*Shh.*" Nicole glanced at the door, hoping he still slept as soundly as he used to. "Just go to bed. It's not a big deal."

"Are you serious? We have every woman's wet dream in our living room." Susan goggled at her. "Have you *seen* him? He's out there sleeping without a shirt on."

Nicole arched her brows.

Susan held her hands up. "I couldn't help noticing. He's laid out like a buffet, and I've been starving for months. You know I haven't dated anyone in forever because of my work schedule."

True. Susan sold pharmaceutical medication and had to travel all the time. She was successful and beautiful, which helped in her sales, but she refused to date any of the doctors she dealt with. Wisely, Nicole had always thought.

"Have you seen his chest?" her roommate whispered in awe. "It's a thing of beauty. Michelangelo would be jealous that he didn't create that. I could lick every —"

"Susan." Nicole winced and sat up, fully awake. "He's my friend."

"Your *friend* is out there half-naked, and I suggest you go check him out because you'll never see a sight like that ever again." She tapped a finger to her lips in thought. "Although he may very well be completely naked. I didn't check under the blanket."

"And you're not going to." Nicole frowned at her roommate. "Go to bed."

"Can I ask him to join me?"

"*No.*"

Susan shrugged, ever pragmatic. "It's okay. I don't mind that you have dibs. It's enough that you brought him here and shared him like this. At least now I know what to aspire to."

"I don't have dibs. It's not like that." Except that he'd kissed her. A shiver went over her body as she remembered the way his lips had claimed hers.

"It's not, is it?" Susan said slyly.

"No, it's not. I'm going back to sleep now." She turned the light off, flounced over, and covered herself with the comforter. "Goodnight."

Her roommate stood there for a long silent minute. Nicole could feel her staring, but then she gave up and left the room.

Nicole sagged in relief.

But sleep was elusive, because her mind churned on Grif. The kiss. That he'd come to her for help.

That he was lying half naked in the living room.

She squeezed her eyes shut, trying not to imagine that. She'd meant it when she told Susan he was her friend. Years of loving someone didn't just go away because you got annoyed at him.

But she was pretty sure friends didn't kiss each other the way he'd kissed her. It'd been like something out of a romance novel, and she was an expert on romance novels.

She tried to feel weird about it. She should have, right? There'd never been anything sexual between them. *Ever.*

Well, maybe once or twice when she was a teenager she'd wondered what it'd be like to be Grif's girlfriend. But that was a logical thing to wonder—they were around each other all the time, and she'd loved him. Of course she'd wonder.

Now at least she didn't have to wonder if he was a good kisser.

Groaning, she muffled her face in her pillow.

Half an hour later, she turned the light back on and reached for her sketchpad and colored pencils. Sometimes drawing helped calm her enough to fall asleep.

Propping herself up on her pillows, she flipped through the book, looking at the previous pages before coming to an empty page. Lately, she'd been drawing lingerie—her own designs based on what she'd seen women appreciate at the store and what she wished they carried. Romantic, sensual pieces that flattered women of all shapes and sizes.

She picked a red pencil out and began sketching, a sexy red number that she'd love to have for herself, the panties with a lush bow in the back that begged to be undone. She added straight brown hair to the model, a birthmark on her hip just like the one she had, and boots. Then, because it wasn't complete, she drew the shadow of a man in the background, with a cowboy hat on his head.

Nicole groaned and ripped the page out of her book. She intended to crumple it, but instead she tucked it under her pillow.

All this was Grif's fault, and he was sleeping

peacefully in the other room, unaware of the torture she was going through. She shoved the covers aside. That was going to change. He wanted a muse? He was about to get one.

She pulled on yoga pants, a tank, and a long-sleeved shirt. Grabbing her puffy jacket, a scarf, and a wool cap, she stuffed her sketchpad, pencils, and an extra notepad in her bag and went to wake him up.

He was on the couch just like Susan had said, bare from the waist up except for a necklace around his neck. Nicole swallowed at the sight, her breath shallow, entranced by the shadowed ridges and the dark goody trail leading under the blanket.

Clearing her throat, she poked him with the tip of one finger. "Wake up."

He murmured and grabbed her hand, bring it to his heart and pulling her down on top of him.

She froze, struck by his warmth and the hard, naked feel of his chest. This wasn't the boy she'd known. He didn't even smell the same as he had when they were teenagers. She leaned down and sniffed. He smelled mysterious and sexy.

Then she really noticed the necklace he wore. Suspended on leather, it was the arrowhead she'd given him before he'd left to make his fortune.

She touched it with her fingertip. They'd been out, walking, talking about the future. He'd been so excited about a gig in Nashville to play with some musician she'd never heard of. She'd been torn between being happy for him and desolate for herself, and then she'd seen the arrowhead on their path. She'd dusted it off and given it to him, to remember her by. To protect him on his path.

He still had it.

She swallowed, not sure what to make of that.

One thing was sure: she needed to get off of him.

He shifted, and her hand brushed his skin. He felt warm—so warm she couldn't help letting her hands steal over his skin. Humming in his sleep, Grif rolled them over and slipped his leg between hers.

He was hard, and it was prominent.

Her heart pounded in her chest. She felt like she was getting away with something she wasn't entitled to, but she couldn't bring herself to move.

It was enough that she managed not to press into his hard-on even more.

His hand smoothed over her hair, and his eyes fluttered open.

Embarrassed to be caught, she took the offensive. "Get off me."

"It seems like you're on me," he said in a sleep-husky voice, but he rolled her back over.

She scrambled off of him, falling on her butt on the floor.

Grif turned the light next to him on and leaned over the couch. "What are you doing, Nicole?"

"Waking you up." She hoisted herself up and straightened her clothes.

"I think you were successful," he said with a dry lilt of his lips, glancing down at the bulge the blanket didn't conceal.

She was *not* going there, no matter how much she wanted to. She cleared her throat. "Get up. We're going to miss it."

"Miss what?" But he swung his legs over the side.

Averting her eyes, she pretended to be busy with her coat and scarf. "Sunrise. It's inspiring."

"I seem to have found plenty of inspiration here," he said, but he stood and reached for his jeans.

"Hurry up," she said, going into the kitchen so she wouldn't be tempted to peek at him. She made coffee and filled two to-go cups before he ambled in to join her. He wore way too many layers of clothes, but it was probably for the best.

She handed him his coffee. "You're driving."

"Okay." He took a sip and exhaled in pleasure. "This is almost worth being woken up pre-dawn."

"You'll thank me later," she said as she led him out of the house.

"Where are we going?"

"Coit Tower. Sunrise is beautiful from up there."

He glanced at her. "You've seen lots of sunrises from Coit Tower?"

Actually, none, but she wasn't going to tell him that. She just shrugged noncommittally and changed the subject. "I brought a notepad for you to write images down. I thought maybe you might find a strain that calls to you."

"Nothing's called to me," he said, subdued, as he unlocked her door.

"We'll get you on track, Grif." She put her hand on his arm. "Trust me."

His hand covered hers and he looked into her eyes. "I do."

They drove to Coit Tower in silence. Because it was so early, no one was on the road, and the parking lot was empty. They got out and went to the statue of Columbus in the middle of the circle.

It was as good a place as any. Nicole sat down on the wide stone ledge around it and extracted the sketchpads from her purse. She handed him the smaller, pocket-sized one along with a pen and took out colored pencils for herself.

"What's this for?" he asked as he accepted it, sitting next to her.

"To write down words or themes that come to you."

"Okay." He pointed at her pencils. "You still draw?"

"Yes. Sort of." She shrugged. "It helps me relax."

"I always thought you were a great artist."

"That's because stick figures were a challenge for you."

"True." He flashed her a self-deprecating smile. "I always expected you to go to art school."

"I went to Arizona State for a couple semesters. I didn't love the art program."

"What do you draw?" He leaned over as if to look at her sketches.

She kept the pad firmly shut. Her drawings were private. "We aren't here to talk about me. We're here to let you be inspired by the sunrise and to talk about your music."

He grimaced. "Watching sunrise is great, but maybe we can leave the music out of it."

"Why aren't you feeling the love?" She faced him, perplexed. "You and your guitar were together all the time in high school. What did you call it?"

"Wanda."

"Right." She rolled her eyes. "Remember that one girl you dated who was so jealous of the relationship you had with Wanda?"

"She was a nut."

"You're the one who names his instruments," she pointed out with a grin.

"Of course I name them. I have an intimate relationship with them." He sat back, stretching his legs in front of him. "My current guitar is named Tallulah, and I haven't touched her in weeks. I don't even feel like touching her, which is really messed up."

"Why?"

He looked at her as if he was trying to gauge what to say. Then he let his eyes shut as he dropped his head back. "I'm tired, Nic."

At first she thought he meant this morning, but she realized he was talking about life in general.

"At first, I thought I was just tired from touring," he continued, "but it's been weeks and I don't feel rejuvenated in any way. I feel a bone-deep weariness." He opened his eyes and gave her a rueful look. "I hate talking like this. I sound like I'm saying 'poor little me, the rock star.'"

She smiled. "It's better than keeping it bottled inside."

He nudged her. "Remember the time you thought you were going to die, because your mom told you that keeping your feelings inside was a sure way to explode and Mrs. Klinger wouldn't let you express in class?"

"Sixth grade was hell." She reclined next to

him, resting against the metal railing behind them. "You wrote that song for me that year. It was your first song, and it was about red Jell-O."

"My first big hit." He chuckled. "I won the talent contest with that song."

"You won the talent contest because even then you were gifted and charismatic." She nodded at the sky. "Sunrise. Write down whatever thoughts you have about it."

He sighed like he was beleaguered schoolboy, but he followed her direction. She listened to the scratch of the pen against the thick paper as orange, pink, and red streaked across the sky.

The vivid hues sparked an idea in her own mind, and she opened her own sketchpad and began drawing a bra with variated colors like the sunrise. She drew quickly, with sparing lines, switching pencils to fill in the colors she wanted. She flipped the page to draw a dusk version with dark colors—midnight blue, purple, and gray.

"You draw underwear?"

She snapped the pad shut. Turning her head, she found Grif right there, so close, watching over her shoulder. "Don't spy on me."

"I'd prefer to call it observing."

She frowned. "Let me see your words then."

"No." He held his sketchpad away from her. "It's private."

"Remember that next time." She put her things back into her purse. "Did you come up with anything good?"

"I wrote a few things down." He sipped his coffee, a bleak look in his eyes. "That's more than I've done in the past several months."

"Don't you have someone who inspires you?" she asked before she could stop herself.

"Like who?"

In for a penny... "Like a woman."

Comprehension dawned on his face. He smiled ruefully. "No, I'm not dating anyone. I haven't in months. Being on tour is hell on a relationship."

"Do you want a relationship?" she asked hesitantly.

"Yes. Eventually." He gazed at the sky. "Like what my parents have, and your parents. You know how close they are. One day, I'd like that."

"But not now?" she pried.

He was quiet for so long that she didn't think

he was going to reply, but then he said, "I've been living the musician's life. Traveling, women throwing themselves at me. I haven't been as bad as some, I hope, but I haven't been a monk. It's a tempting lifestyle when you're in your early twenties. But, yes, given the right situation, I could see myself with one woman forever."

Nicole tried to picture the type of woman who'd be with him. Tall and blond, like that model he'd dated last year, according to the celebrity magazines. She frowned.

He turned his head to focus on her. "What about you? What do you want from life?"

"I just want to live my passion." That was the line she gave anyone who questioned her direction—or lack thereof—in life.

Grif stared at her. She wondered what he was thinking—his gaze was hooded and she couldn't read his thoughts. It made her uncomfortable.

But then he took her hand in his, holding it loosely. "This was a good idea, Nicole. Thank you."

She looked at where they were joined. She knew she should pull her hand away, but it was just a friendly gesture.

Only when was the last time one of her "friends" tried to hold her hand?

Right.

Still, even as she told herself to disengage, she couldn't do it. It was nice, sitting with him as the sun streaked pink across the sky. "I missed you," she heard the words slip from her mouth.

He rubbed his thumb along hers. "I missed you, too, Nicole."

Chapter Five

RACHEL STOPPED BY her French class after school, to ask Madame Roche a question. She could care less about conjugating the verb *avoir* in past perfect tense — she cared that it'd take a long time to explain because her teacher didn't know how to give a concise answer. By the time Roche was finished, the ¬*sons of anarchy* would be gone and Rachel's locker would be clear.

After ten minutes of explanation, she managed to extricate herself from her teacher's clutches. She walked down the hall, head lowered, just in case. Before she rounded the corner to her locker, she peered around the corner to check.

The coast was clear.

Her shoulders relaxed, and she headed straight to her locker. She just needed to switch one book and then she could leave. The quicker she was in and out, the better. She fumbled with the padlock, exhaling when it clicked open. She pulled the book out of her bag and looked into her locker.

Then she froze.

Dangling from the middle of the small space was a pair of yellow briefs with SpongeBob on them. A note was pinned to them: *We found these and figured they were yours. You're welcome.*

She tugged them down and shoved them in her bag. This had to stop. She'd show them. She'd get better underwear than the tacky stuff they wore.

There was that store across from Grounds for Thought: Romantic Notions. She'd go there and get expensive underwear that'd make them jealous. Then she'd shove the yellow briefs down their throats.

"Hey."

Slamming the door shut, she whirled around to find Aaron Hawke leaning against Madison's locker. Did he see the SpongeBob underwear? Her cheeks burned.

"Are you okay?" he asked. "You have a funny look on your face."

"I'm fine." She hugged her bag closer and began walking toward the exit.

"Uh-oh." He followed her, his long legs easily keeping pace with her brisk city-girl walk. "Whenever people say they're fine, they're usually anything but."

She glanced at him. "I'm not sure why you'd care."

He smiled. "I know, but I do."

His smile did something funny to the pit of her stomach. Her tongue suddenly felt too big in her mouth, so she walked faster to cover it up.

"Where are you headed?" he asked, seemingly not bothered by the fact that she was practically running.

She shrugged, feeling her face go red again as she thought about Aaron Hawke knowing she was going to Romantic Notions. "Nowhere."

"Want to get hot chocolate?"

She stopped abruptly and goggled at him. "Like a date?"

He laughed. "Don't look so excited."

Shaking her head, she said, "I have an errand to take care of."

"Ouch." Aaron put a hand over his heart. "You know how to take a guy down a peg. Can I at least walk you wherever you're going?"

The thought of one of the hottest boys in school knowing she was going to buy underwear embarrassed her. She shook her head emphatically as she edged away from him. "That's not an excellent idea. I, um, I'll see you tomorrow."

Before he could say anything, she hurried off. She turned left on a street, walking away from the lingerie store, before doubling back on another street. As she approached Romantic Notions, she checked to make sure no one she knew was around. Seeing no one but a woman pushing a stroller, Rachel rushed in and closed the door firmly behind her.

Heart pounding, she looked around the store. There was underwear everywhere: hanging from little padded ivory hangers, covering tables in colorful piles, and spilling out of dresser drawers. She did a slow circle, amazed. This was a whole world she hadn't known existed. Where did she start?

A lady in a short skirt, sweater, tights, and boots came out from the back. "Hey there. Feel free to look around, and if you need help just give me a shout."

"Thank you," Rachel murmured, ducking her head and moving to the opposite side of the room. She stopped in front of a lacy red bra and matching underwear.

Red was grown up. Standing in front of it, she frowned at the bra. It had a hole right in the middle of it. What good was it if it wasn't going to cover anything?

She moved on to the black bra next to it. It seemed whole, and a little more protective, with thin black straps that criss-crossed all across the front. Black was way grown-up. Addison wore a lot of black.

"That's really nice on," the sales lady said, rummaging in a dresser on the other side of the store. "But if you're looking for a bra, I have one over here I think would look fabulous on you."

Rachel looked at the bra and panties that the lady brought over to her. It didn't have straps or thin frilly lace. It was black with tiny pink polka dots and a pink bow at the center. The underwear was matching, with a bow in front.

"I brought you the boy shorts, but I have matching thongs, too." The lady smiled. "I love the boy shorts, and with your long slim legs they're going to look fantastic."

"Really?" She tried to remember if Addison or Madison wore boy shorts.

"Try it," the woman encouraged her. "They'll look hot. The dressing room is back that way. My name is Nicole, if you need help."

Nodding, she dragged her feet to the curtain Nicole pointed at. She shrugged off her bag and stripped down to her underwear. Turning, she studied herself in the mirror.

As much as she hated to admit it, the —sons were right: her underwear was ugly. Wrinkling her nose, she took them off and put on the set the saleswoman had given her.

"How are you doing in there?" The curtain swept aside and Nicole popped her head in.

Rachel gasped, covering herself.

"Let me see." Like it was nothing, Nicole moved Rachel's arms and surveyed the bra. Then she twirled her finger. "Turn around. We need to adjust it a little."

Mortified, she stood silently as the woman tightened and adjusted straps. "That's the way it's supposed to fit," Nicole said with a nod. "Look now."

The quicker she humored the woman, the sooner she'd leave, so Rachel turned and glanced in the mirror. Then she did a double-take. "I have breasts."

Nicole grinned. "The power of a good bra. Do you see the back here? It should fit straight across your back. Your other bra was riding up."

She'd thought that was just the way bras were. She wondered if her mom had known that. "How did you know?"

"I could tell. It's what I do. And those boy shorts really do look amazing on you."

She looked down. They rode lower on her hips than her briefs, and they made her feel strange, but in a good way. She blushed, imagining Aaron looking at them. "I'll buy them," she said impulsively.

"Good decision." The sales lady patted her shoulder. "I'll meet you outside."

She got dressed, reluctantly putting on her

old underwear. She covered it quickly with her T-shirt and sweater to hide it and tugged her jeans up.

When she walked out of the dressing room, the saleswoman was talking to a man. Rachel could only see him from the back, but she wondered why he was in San Francisco. Based on his hat and boots, he was obviously a cowboy.

He looked relaxed, the way he leaned against the counter with one boot crossed over the other. Which was kind of cool, because *she* was uncomfortable in the lingerie store and she was a girl. If she were a guy, she'd be doubly uncomfortable. He seemed right at home.

Was he buying underwear for his girlfriend? Was Nicole his girlfriend? She wondered what it'd be like to have a boyfriend, or to have him buy things for her, especially private things like underwear. She tried to picture Aaron in here. He'd actually be relaxed, just like the cowboy.

The sales lady looked around the guy, her hand outstretched. "I'll take that, honey."

The man turned around and smiled at her.

Rachel froze midstep, her breath catching like

she'd been knocked in the chest. Griffin Chase. He was Griffin Chase.

She opened her mouth, wanting to tell him how her mom loved his music and used to listen to it all the time. That his music saved her after her mom died. She'd been so alone, but when she listened to his songs it was like had a friend who understood her. Whenever she felt really alone, she'd put his albums on repeat and she could almost feel her mom still with her. But her tongue got all mangled in her mouth again.

He turned his attention to Nicole. "I should go so you can work. See you later, Nic?"

"Do I have a choice?" But the saleswoman said it with a hint of a smile.

"You always have a choice."

The lady rolled her eyes. "Get out of here before you cause a riot."

He winked at the lady and then turned his smile on Rachel.

She gasped. He was so much better looking than on his album covers or the poster in Madison's locker. She swallowed, reaching out her hand. "Griffin Chase," she croaked.

"See?" the saleswoman said.

He leaned forward, a finger to his lips, looking right into her eyes. "Shh. Don't tell anyone."

Rachel shook her head in awe. "I won't," she managed to say this time.

With another smile, he left the store. She watched him put his sunglasses on and head down the street. Did he live in Laurel Heights?

Nicole sighed. "Another conquest."

Rachel turned. "What?"

"Never mind." She shook her head, smiling gently. "If you like this set, there's another in lime that'd look great with your skin."

"Yes, please. I'll take both." She took out the emergency credit card her dad had given her. If there was ever an emergency, it was this. "Is Griffin Chase your boyfriend?"

"*No.*" Nicole made a face like the thought was disgusting. "We used to be best friends in high school."

"Really?" Rachel tried to think of having someone like him as her best friend. For some reason she thought of Aaron. "So you're not dating him?"

"Dating someone popular like him may seem

like a great idea. He's hot and successful, and it'd be exciting. But there are downsides."

Maybe, but it seemed like the respect she'd get from dating the best musician on the planet would be worth it. "What downsides?"

"More than I could list. Like that I get roped into helping with his music when he gets stuck." Nicole's smile took the sting out of her words.

"He gets stuck?" That was what *she* felt like. She hadn't been able to write anything since her mom's funeral.

The saleslady shrugged. "Every creative person gets confused at some point. Sometimes you just need a friend to point you in the right direction."

Rachel nodded. She wished she could be Griffin Chase's friend. How awesome would that be? And then she could help him with his songs — not the music part, but with the lyrics. If she knew him, she'd give him the poem she'd written for her mom.

Nicole handed over the little burgundy bag. "Come back in a week. We'll have new pieces you'll like."

She nodded, taking the little bag home. Rachel

stopped abruptly on the sidewalk as a thought occurred to her: if Nicole and Griffin Chase were friends, he probably hung out at Romantic Notions a lot. Meaning if she went there more often, she might run into him.

Meaning maybe she could give him her mom's poem.

Her heart beat to hard that she thought it was going to jump out of her chest. Her mom would have been beyond excited to have Griffin Chase sing a song dedicated to her.

She ran all the way home, bursting through the door and sprinting up the stairs to her room. Dumping her bag's contents onto the bed, she looked for the journal. She scrambled to open it, searching for the loose piece of paper.

Here. She smoothed it open and read it. *You moved away…*

Closing her eyes, she imagined Griffin Chase singing it. It'd be perfect.

It was one last thing she could do for her mom — the only way to keep her alive.

It'd be a great way to get back at the *—sons of anarchy*.

Rachel pictured their faces when they heard Griffin Chase used her poem for song lyrics. Especially Madison's. It'd be the best thing *ever*.

She flopped onto her bed, hugging the paper to her chest. She'd get him to do it. She'd get him to use it for a song, and it'd be beautiful in so many ways.

Chapter Six

HIS PHONE RANG as he was jogging through the Presidio. Grif checked the screen. Roddy.

He had no desire to talk to his manager. He knew exactly how the conversation would go. He'd say hi, and Roddy would ask him where the hell the new songs were and why he wasn't in the recording studio.

Except in the past couple days, Grif had realized he was a masochist. Why else would he insist on living with Nicole? It was pure torture. He couldn't write anything when he spent every minute of the entire day thinking about kissing her — and more.

And being a masochist, Grif stopped and answered the phone.

Before he could say even a syllable, his manager jumped down his throat. "Where are you?"

"I miss you, too." He walked around, free hand on his hip, trying to breathe.

"Cut out the cute act, Chase. You're in serious hot water here."

He was always in serious hot water with his manager. Roddy had always been stricter with him than his dad had been. He guessed Roddy had repped a lot of musicians who had gone down the path of alcohol and drugs. It was easy to do—the phrase *sex and drugs and rock 'n roll* wasn't coined just because.

While he had a moment in his career where the sex was really attractive, he'd backed off on all of that. It was about the music, first and foremost. Without it, he'd be nothing.

Which was why he was there, with Nicole. That last night of his tour, he'd been so tempted to chuck it all. But even in that dark moment he'd known that wasn't really the answer.

"Well?" his manager asked in his typical, impatient tone. "What's going on? Where are you? What are you doing?"

"I'm running," Grif replied, knowing it'd infuriate the man.

"That's not what I was asking," Roddy yelled into his ear. "Where the fu—eff are you?"

He grinned. Roddy's daughter was approaching adolescence, so he was especially conscious of his language, probably because his wife made it necessary. She'd told him that for every curse word, he had to pay a hundred dollars into her shopping fund. In the past year, she'd had to convert a second closet into a space just for her shoes. "You know I'm not going to tell you where I am. You'd send the Coast Guard to retrieve me."

"Fu—eff yeah, I would. All shi—crap's hit the fan here."

"That's what I pay you to handle."

"I won't have anything to handle if you don't have a contract."

Grif stopped pacing. "What?"

"The studio execs are getting nervous. You're supposed to be recording now, but you aren't anywhere to be found, and they haven't seen any music from you."

He raked his hair back, missing his cowboy hat. Wearing it as a disguise started as a joke, because the media called him the Urban Cowboy, but he kind of liked it. It made him harder to recognize.

It made him a hero, when he hadn't felt especially heroic lately.

He shook his head. "I'm working on it. That's the entire purpose of this trip, to give me space to figure out the rest of the album."

"Tell me you have something."

"I have something," he lied.

"Liar." Roddy growled. "Chase, you're giving me ulcers. You know this, right? My stomach is bleeding because of you."

He sighed, thinking of the notebook Nicole had given him to jot down ideas. So far it was a third full of stick figures with swords and Nicole's name over and over. "I'll get the songs done, and they'll be good. When have I ever let you down?"

"There's always a first time." There was a pause. "I wasn't kidding about the execs. They're nervous because you've suddenly disappeared. In their eyes, you're off somewhere having sex and shooting heroine into your eyeballs. You need to give me something soon, or they may cut you loose before you become a liability."

"I'm not going to become a liability."

"You know that. I know that. But the execs don't know shi—crap." Roddy cursed under his breath. "Damn it, that one was close."

Grif smiled. "You're a good man, Roddy. I won't let you down."

His manager sighed. "Where did you say you are?"

"I didn't, but that was a good try. Talk to you later."

"Damn it—"

Grif hung up, tucked his phone away, and started running back.

The thing about running was that it gave you time to think. Most of the time, he liked the space it gave him. Today he could have done without it. The pressure to produce a hit album wasn't atypical; the desire to stay with Nicole was. The sooner he had his song, the sooner he'd have to leave.

Picking up the pace, he headed back toward her apartment. He wasn't ready to leave. There was something between him and Nicole, something more than the simple friendship they'd known as teenagers. He wanted to know what that was and how deep it went.

He rounded the block and slowed to a walk the rest of the way to her apartment. Susan kept unusual times, leaving early one day and late the next, but she was always out midday. Nicole's hours were steady: she'd leave a little before eleven and return home after seven.

The apartment should have felt empty while they were gone, but the women always left him unintentional reminders of their presence. He smiled as he almost stumbled over the calf-high boots Nicole had kicked off in the living room the night before.

She liked all sorts of boots, short and high. He had to admit his favorites were the long red ones she'd been wearing at the wedding. At night when he couldn't sleep he thought about her wearing those boots and not much else.

No, that never helped him fall asleep.

Stripping out of his shirt, Grif headed to her bathroom to take a shower. As he walked through her room, he noticed one of her notebooks lying on her bed.

He stopped, staring at it. He shouldn't invade her privacy, but he knew nothing was going to stop him either. She'd been secretive about her drawings that morning they'd gone to Coit Tower, and he was curious. Nicole used to draw all the time, for as long as he could remember, and she'd always been good.

He crossed the room and opened it.

It was filled with page after page of sketches of women of different sizes and shapes. Some were standing, some reclining, but all wore beautiful lingerie that enhanced their shape.

He flipped through a second time, slowly, entranced. He didn't know much about lingerie except how to take it off, but to his untrained eyes Nicole's designs were exquisite. Romantic and colorful, exciting and flattering.

She had a gift.

He especially liked the one on the last page. Sheer black with a touch of frill, he could see Nicole in it. With her boots, of course.

Squeezing his eyes shut, he shook his head. It was so wrong picturing Nicole's nipples peeking through the see-through lace — and such a turn-on.

He quickly shut the notebook and took care to make sure it was in the same spot where he'd found it. Was she pursuing lingerie design and just being quiet about it? His mom hadn't said anything to him about it, and she was tight with Nicole's mom.

If he knew Nicole, it was more likely she hadn't committed to the idea. She'd always flitted from one interest to the next. As a kid, it'd been cute. Now, seeing her designs and how incredible they were, it made him sad.

He went into the shower, not sure what to do about it. Not sure if Nicole would appreciate him doing anything about it, and that was the hardest pill to swallow.

Chapter Seven

"BABY HAS A new bra," Madison cooed in the locker room.

Rachel stilled as she hooked one of her new bras. The pleasure she'd felt all day, feeling pretty underneath where no one could see, began to dim, and that pissed her off. Her new bras were fabulous — Nicole would reassure her of that. And Nicole was the one who was so beautiful and hung out with Griffin Chase. She was the one to emulate, not sheep like the evil *-sons*.

"She actually has boobs," Addison said, joining in with her fake laugh.

That was it. Whirling around, she flashed a sticky-sweet smile at the two girls. "I can give you the name of the store, if you want to do something about *that*." She nodded at pityingly at Madison's chest.

Her nemesis's face went so red Rachel thought she was going to explode. For a second she was afraid they were going to retaliate, but then the PE teacher came into the locker and blew her shrill whistle. "Get going, ladies. You only have five minutes left to shower and go to your next class."

The ¬*sons of anarchy* shot Rachel a glare and turned their back on her.

A victory. She smiled softly to herself. Wait till Griffin Chase used her poem in a song. Then they'd bow down.

But she wasn't going to hang around to let the girls gather the one wit they shared. Deciding to forgo the shower to avoid giving them a target, she got dressed before they came back.

As she left the locker room, another girl tugged her arm. Rachel stiffened, turning to look at her. It was Lydia, with the small glasses and big lips, who sat next to her in chemistry. "That was brilliant. Madison and her boobs have had it coming for a long time. I only wish I were recording it so I could put the whole thing on Youtube."

What a horror that'd have been. Rachel shrugged off the girl's hold. "It was nothing."

"It was socially *significant*." Lydia blinked at her. "Do you know how many girls would have liked to stand up to Madison and her crony but haven't had the guts? You're like a superhero."

"I can't be a superhero. I don't have a cape." She gave her a polite smile and walked out of locker room.

One more period with Madison, she told herself, trudging to English. She'd almost made it inside and safely to her seat when she felt someone fall in step next to her.

Looking up, she relaxed when she saw Aaron. "Oh, it's just you."

"I'm excited to see you, too." He grinned at her.

She rolled her eyes. "I didn't mean it like that. I thought you were someone else."

"Tell me you didn't think I was Matt West, because that pisses me off."

Matt West was probably the only guy in school who was more popular than Aaron. She could tell he was joking about that, especially because she saw them hanging out all the time. But she bit her lip to keep from smiling. She didn't want to encourage him.

He took her bag from her shoulder and slung it over his. "Who'd you think I was?" he asked as he began to walk slowly to class.

She pointed at her bag. "What are you doing? I can carry that myself."

"But this way you have to talk to me." He flashed her his cute dimpled smile. "So who did you think I was?"

"The —*sons of anarchy.*"

"Excuse me?" He stopped and stared at her.

She sighed, forced to stop, too. "Madison and Addison."

He threw his head back and laughed, so loud that everyone around them gawked.

"Shh," she hissed at him.

"That's just too perfect." Shaking his head, he wiped his eyes.

She grabbed her bag from him while he was still laughing. "They deserve that nickname. They're horrible."

"They are," he agreed.

She looked at him suspiciously. "Really?"

"I've seen how they treat you. They've been acting mean to every new girl since kindergarten, but if it makes you feel more special, they're especially mean to you."

"Great," she muttered, hitching her bag closer.

"They feel threatened by you."

She rolled her eyes. "Right."

"They do." He touched her arm. "You're smarter and prettier than they are."

Her stomach twitched nervously and she froze, not sure what to do or how to reply.

Aaron just smiled at her. "Let's go inside so we're not late."

Nodding mutely, she followed him in.

She spent all of class staring at his head, wondering why he was so nice to her. She had no answer for it.

Rachel stared at the friend request, not sure what to do.

Aaron Hawke wants to be friends on Facebook.

Why? He had plenty of friends. He didn't

need her. Boys like him didn't hang out with social pariahs like her.

She pulled out the lyrics she'd written and looked at them. She'd sat outside Romantic Notions today but there wasn't any sign of Griffin Chase. She *needed* to talk to him. She knew if she asked him to use even one line of her poem it'd be enough to change everything.

Her email pinged with a new message. Frowning, she looked at her inbox.

It was from her dad. She stared at it, stunned. He hadn't sent her an email since—

Well, it'd been a really long time.

She clicked it open.

To: rachel_rose@gmail.com

From: jim.rosenbaum@valleytechnology.com

Subject: In case you don't remember, this is your father.

Dear Rachel,

I thought maybe you and I can go out to dinner one of these nights. Maybe

Friday? We can catch a movie afterward.

The thing is, I never see you. I know this is my fault, and I'd like to fix it. Our world was crushed after your mom died. It was my job to put it back together, but I didn't know how to do it. I thought I lost everything when Wendy died, but I was wrong. I still have the world, because I still have you.

I'm sorry. I should have tried harder. I want to change this. Maybe you can meet me halfway? I think your mom would have wanted that.

Love,
Dad

Rachel stared at the letter. There were so many feelings inside her—all of the stages of grief that the therapist had taught her, only all at once.

But the two biggest were sadness and anger.

He didn't know what mom wanted. Mom wouldn't have wanted to move to San Francisco—

everything was in New York. Mom would have hated it here, with all the slow-walking, happy people on the streets. She'd have hated the —*sons* as much as Rachel did. And you couldn't even buy a decent bagel here.

The only thing Mom would have wanted was a special song for her, sung by Griffin Chase. Rachel knew that, and she was going to make it happen.

She swallowed her tears. She wouldn't cry. Tears didn't help. They only made you feel sick. She had to do something.

She deleted the email.

She'd find Griffin Chase. She would.

Chapter Eight

"Lottie Chase called me yesterday and told me Grif had been back to visit," her mom said. "Actually, she mentioned that he was on his way to San Francisco."

He'd told her he'd gone home to see his parents. He'd driven the old tank he'd lovingly restored in high school. She couldn't believe he still had that old Chevy. He'd told her a true love lasts a lifetime. It had to be true love if he manufactured excuses for road trips just to drive it. "Yes, he showed up the night of Valentine and Ethan's wedding."

"To visit you."

Switching on the light in the storeroom, Nicole shook her head at her mom's eager tone. "It's not like that, Mom."

"What is it like, sweetheart?"

"His creativity's flagging and he needs some encouragement. That's all." She opened a box, looking for tissue paper.

"And sometime in the past year you've become a creativity coach?"

"With all the different jobs I've had, it shouldn't be such a surprise," Nicole replied dryly.

"You'll find your way, Nicole." Her mom's voice was firm and confident.

If only she could feel that sure about it. Her parents always reassured her that everyone had a purpose, it just took some people longer to find theirs. At this rate, Nicole was going to be in her eighties before she figured out what she wanted out of life.

"Are you still drawing?" he mom asked.

This again. She sighed. She thought of the sketchpad she had out on the counter. Sometimes when it got slow, she worked on designs. "A little bit."

"You're a talented artist, sweetheart. Maybe you should go back to art school. I hear there are excellent schools in San Francisco."

"And be poor and without means all my life?" She gripped the phone between her ear and shoulder and lifted a box away to get to the one behind it. "No thanks."

"You're so talented. It's just a shame to waste it."

"You're my mom. You're supposed to think I'm talented." *A-ha—found it.* She withdrew a stack of burgundy tissue. "Remember how Lottie used to post Grif's drawings on the refrigerator?"

Mom laughed. "I felt so bad for the poor boy. His drawings were awful."

"He couldn't even draw hangman." Nicole grinned, remembering how much he'd hated art. But he was a genius with music and had always known what he wanted.

"I think it's fantastic that Grif is visiting you," her mom said. "You two were so close at one time, it'll be good for you to get to know each other again. I always thought you two were meant for each other."

Nicole sighed as she kicked a box out of her way. "It's not like that, Mom."

"What is it like, Nicole?"

She had no idea. That kiss, the handholding, the flutter of anticipation in her belly whenever he walked in the room... It defied reason.

The front door bell chimed, proverbially saving her. "Mom, I have a customer. I have to go."

"Love you, sweetheart. Your dad sends his love, too. Give Grif a kiss from me."

Her lips weren't going anywhere near Griffin Chase, but she just murmured in assent and disconnected the call. Taking the stack of tissue paper, she went back out to the front.

Bull, Ethan's friend, stood at the counter, looking like his namesake in a china shop. He was big, but his size was magnified when he was surrounded by such femininity. "This is a surprise," she said as she carried the tissue behind the counter.

"Hey, girl." Bull flipped a page of her sketchpad. "Did you draw these?"

Blushing, she quickly confiscated it, closing it and stowing it under the register. "They're nothing really."

"They don't look like nothing, but, hey, what do I know?" He shrugged and handed her a thermal to-go cup. "I brought you a smoothie."

"That's so"—she tried to find a word as she accepted the cup—"nice. Thank you."

He laughed, deep from his belly. "At the gym, I'm kind of known for my smoothies. Try it. You'll like it."

Uncapping it, she took a tentative sip. She blinked in surprise. "This is good."

"Told ya." Grinning, he leaned on the counter and looked around. "Love the digs. If I knew you worked here, I'd have come sooner."

"You didn't know me sooner. We only met at the wedding." She tipped her head and frowned at him. "How *did* you know I worked here?"

"Valentine told me." He shook his head. "She had some crazy idea that you and I would be good together."

Nicole shook her head. Thank goodness Valentine had decided to stop matchmaking. She really had no skill for it. "Valentine means well."

Bull pointed a finger at her. "I meant it when I said you're not my type. You're too young and too scrawny."

"Scrawny?" She couldn't help grinning.

"I like my women with a little meat on them. I

like something to hold on to." He looked around. "I'm not dating anyone right now, but maybe when I am, I can come back and buy her things. That green bra over there rocks."

She looked at where he pointed, to the sassy emerald satin demi and garter. "That's really nice on."

"Which brings me to the reason I came by. Griffin Chase."

Nicole groaned. "Not you, too."

He held his hands up. "I just wanted to make sure you were okay."

"Did I look that disgruntled to see him?"

"No, you looked wary but hopeful, which is why I wanted to check on you." Bull leaned in, his finger right in her face. "He may be one of the greatest musicians since Springsteen, but that doesn't mean he's allowed to walk all over people."

"Grif isn't going to walk all over me." Touched, she took Bull's hand and squeezed it. "You're sweet for caring."

"Of course I care." He puffed his chest out. "You're the best girl of my best man's best girl."

"I think I actually understood that," she said with a grin.

He chucked her with his fist, surprisingly gently for someone who beat up other men for a living. "It's my smoothie. It adds brain power."

"I'll be sure to drink all of it then." Hopefully it also added fortitude, to give her the strength to resist the temptation of having Grif so close.

Chapter Nine

RACHEL HATED CHEMISTRY. It was a lot of letters and numbers jumbled together and none of it made sense.

But lately she had another reason to dread going: Aaron was in her class.

She dragged her feet down the hall, wishing she could skip. But Laurel Heights High was strict about attendance, so she wanted to save getting in trouble for when she really needed to play hooky.

Looking at the ground, she scuffled into class and slinked onto her seat at the back lab table. She hoped no one noticed her.

But her hopes were dashed when Lydia, who sat next to her, looked up from her textbook and said brightly, "Hey Rachel."

Mumbling something in return, she tucked

her chin into her chest as she got out a notebook —
not the one her mom got her — and worked on the
lyrics she wanted to give Griffin Chase when she
met him again.

Most people would have gotten the clue. Lydia wasn't most people. "Did you finish the homework for today? If you want to check your answers, I have mine here."

Coming from anyone else, the offer would have
been a kiss-up. Lydia, though, was just enthusi-
astic about science and friendly despite Rachel's
lack of interest.

She didn't get it. She'd have thought Lydia
was just clueless, but after sitting next to her for
weeks, she realized Lydia was just *nice*. "I'm okay.
Thanks," she added as an afterthought.

"No worries!" Lydia flashed her perfect white
teeth and then asked the geeky boy who sat across
from them about some sort of compound.

Rachel watched him light up with nerdy interest. Shaking her head, she checked out the rest of
class as the final bell rang.

Aaron Hawke stared at her from across the
room.

She looked away quickly, her heart beating. She let her gaze dart over to him again. His lips were curved in a smile this time, like he knew she had a secret, and he knew what it was.

Blushing, she turned away and caught Madison giving her the evil eye. Confused, Rachel looked away.

Praeger, their chem teacher, clacked a stirrer against a flask. "Settle down, class. Today we're going to delve into the scintillating world of exothermic reactions, so I'll assign your new lab partners and we can get to it, huh?"

Frowning, she turned to Lydia. "New lab partners? I thought we were paired for the rest of the year?"

Looking perplexed, Lydia lifted her hands up. "Apparently not?"

The teacher began reading names in tandem. "Ostrinsky and Parma, James and Brown, Sardoff and White, Rosenbaum and Hawke, Fishman and—"

Hawke? Her gaze jerked up to Aaron's. He just grinned at her.

Lydia leaned over. "You're with Aaron Hawke.

You don't know it yet, but you're so lucky. Not only is he cute, but he's the smartest boy in class."

"I'm something," she said, gathering up her books. "I'm just not sure lucky is the right word."

"You're right." Grinning, Lydia handed her her bag. "Especially if Madison retaliates."

"Madison?"

"She's got a wicked crush on him."

Rachel stopped packing her things. "What?"

"I thought you knew." Lydia blinked at her owlishly. "That's the reason Madison and her crony have been giving you such a hard time. Although I don't know why you have to pay for the fact that he likes you."

"He doesn't like me," she said automatically. She glanced at Madison, who had *kill* written all over her face.

"Uh-huh," Lydia said with a sarcastic roll of her eyes.

She slowly made her way across the room, conscious of Madison's death glare as she dropped the bag and perched on the seat next to Aaron.

"Hey." He nudged her with his elbow. "You

could look a little less like you're being led to the gas chamber."

She gave him a baleful look. "I'm in chemistry."

"But look who your lab partner is."

"Feeling modest today?" she mumbled, leaving her notebook closed so he wouldn't see her lyrics.

"I'm but your humble servant." He pushed the assignment pages between them. "Should we start on this?"

Rachel stared at the print outs and felt panic at the thought of completely bombing in front of him.

"Chemistry isn't your subject, is it?" he asked gently as he hooked up the Bunsen burner.

She glanced at him sharply. "Why would you say that?"

"The look of utter terror on your face." He grinned and held out a test tube. "Want to do this?"

"No."

He laughed, his hair flopping back, his dimples cute. The sound of his laughter made her feel warm, even if it was at her expense.

Flushing, she tried to not notice the curious

looks from the students around them—or the hatred from Madison.

"I'll make a deal with you," he said.

"What sort of deal?"

"I'll carry us through this project if you help me with my English term paper. I suck at writing."

"Writing is so easy though."

"For you maybe, but for me it's like pulling teeth." He turned to her. "What do you say? We can work after school."

"Not today," she said automatically, blushing when she realized he didn't mean to start right away. "It's just I have plans already today."

"What plans?"

She was going to Romantic Notions to wait for Griffin Chase. She *had* to give him the poem. She'd gone the past few days after school and waited for him until that lady who was his best friend closed the shop and went home, but he hadn't shown up yet. Rachel knew it was only a matter of time though. All the news sources reported that he was on a private island, working on his next album, but she'd seen him with her own eyes. It hadn't been some weird doppelgänger either.

"Rachel." Aaron waved his hand in front of her face.

She frowned at him. "What?"

He rolled his eyes. "Okay, don't tell me what you've got going on. Just tell me when we can meet."

The lingerie store closed by seven each night. "Would after dinner be okay?"

He shrugged. "My parents are never home, so whatever works for you is great. Will your parents care?"

She swallowed the sudden lump in her throat. "It's just my dad, and he's always at work."

"Are your parents divorced?"

The tears sprang up so suddenly they startled her as much as they did Aaron. She ducked her head and pretended to search for a pencil as she blinked them away.

A Kleenex appeared in her line of vision. She looked up, to find Aaron looking contrite and worried.

No one had cared about her feelings in so long.

"I shouldn't have been so nosy," he said softly.

She shook her head, taking the tissue and blotting the edges of her eyes. "It's not your fault. It's just my mom died. It was a year and a half ago, but still."

"Is that why you moved to San Francisco?"

She nodded, not wanting to tell him about getting drunk at the party. She felt stupid enough on her own about that. "My dad thought we needed a change of scenery and a fresh start," she said with only a small amount of bitterness.

Aaron made a face. "That sucks. You must miss your friends."

She did, but they apparently didn't miss her. Not even Diana had texted her back.

"You were close to your mom?" he asked as he handed her a set of goggles.

"She was my best friend." She glanced at him. "I know that sounds weird but we were really close. She was awesome. Beautiful and talented. She was an editor for a big publisher."

"No wonder you love English."

She frowned. "I don't love English."

"Yeah, you do." He struck the flint and lit the burner. "You pretend like you don't care and aren't paying attention, but you do. I can tell by the look of disgust on your face when you disagree with something Michael says."

"I don't have a look of disgust," she protested.

"It's like this." He lowered his head and scrunched his face.

A rusty laugh escaped her lips before she could bite it back. "It's not."

"I'll hold up a mirror next time I see it." He grinned at her. "Who do you have dinner with usually?"

It took her a moment to follow the shift in the conversation. She shrugged. It seemed pathetic to say that she usually ate a bowl of cereal standing up at the counter.

"Then maybe you can come over for dinner first before we work on my essay," he said, lining up the test tubes. "I make a mean frozen pizza."

"Maybe." She handed Aaron tongs, realizing her lips felt funny. It took a moment before she realized she was smiling.

Chapter Ten

"RIGHT AT THIS moment, Valentine and the Hulk are *getting it on.*" Marley winked as she lifted her coffee cup. "Have you thought about that?"

"I try not to think about my friends getting it on," Nicole said, shaking her head and returning her attention to her sketchpad. On impulse, she gave the woman in her drawing red hair, for Valentine, because her friend would look awesome in this romantic pink bustier.

"But she's getting it on with *the Hulk*. It boggles my mind."

"They're on their honeymoon, but they may not be getting it on." As she drew in pink ties on the sides of the panties, she wondered what Marley would say if she knew Griffin Chase was hanging out in her apartment. Or that he'd kissed her and held her hand.

"Are you serious? Did you see the way he looked at her? At the wedding, I seriously thought he was going to eat her up."

"I know. It was so sweet. That was a romantic night."

"What are you doing?"

"Just doodling." She closed the sketchpad and put the pencils aside before her friend peeked.

Marley tapped the table, staring at her expectantly. "So..."

She shook her head. "What?"

"What the hell, Nicole?" Her friend threw her hands in the air. "Are you going to tell me why Griffin Chase came and pulled you out of the reception or not? I've been waiting days. Do you know how hard it's been to respect your space and not demand an explanation?"

She sighed. "You recognized Grif?"

"Is there anyone in the world who wouldn't recognize him?"

"I'm sure not everyone is a fan of his music."

"Forget his music. The man is hot. Have you

looked at him? He oozes charisma and sex. He swaggered into the room and stole every woman's breath, in a cowboy hat no less. He should have just looked ridiculous."

Nicole frowned.

"Were *you* immune?" Marley narrowed her gaze with suspicion. "Don't lie to me."

She lowered her gaze to her teacup. She normally drank coffee, but she'd thought she'd try chamomile tea. If there were ever a time when she needed to be calmed, it was now with Grif back. "It's not like that between me and Grif."

"That's not how he looked at you," Marley said.

Her belly fluttered, but it was probably indigestion. "How did he look at me?"

"Like you were a Stradivarius and he wanted to run his hands all over you."

She swallowed. "He plays guitar, not the violin."

Marley raised her brow.

"He kissed me," Nicole blurted, unable to hold it back even though she knew she should. "He came back into my life, told me he wanted me to help with his music, and then he kissed me."

"Wait a second." Marley held up a hand, thinking. Finally she shook her head. "Okay, I'm not sure which of those statements to attack first."

"Tell me about it." She slumped on her elbows, her chin resting on her hands. "I've been grappling with it all for days now."

"How do you even know him?"

"He was my best friend, but that was before he became a rock star."

"I can't believe you never told us you were friends with Griffin Chase. Valentine's going to kill you when she finds out."

"Grif and I aren't friends anymore. We lost touch ages ago. I never expected to see him again."

"But he kissed you."

"Yes." She leaned forward, speaking quickly. "I don't understand that. He shows up out of nowhere, kisses me, and then doesn't try it again."

"Are you upset because he kissed you, or because he hasn't kissed you again?"

She pursed her lips. "Both."

Marley nodded. "I would be, too."

"But he's just going to leave, so it's better that he doesn't, isn't it?"

"There's no chance he'd stay?"

"Music is his life. He may not feel it right now, but performing is what makes him happy."

"I read he ended a tour a few months ago."

She nodded. "He's burnt out. He needs to finish his next album and he wants me to help him remember his passion for music. He thinks I'm some sort of muse."

"How far are you willing to go to inspire him?" Marley held her hand up. "Before you get into all the reasons why you shouldn't get involved in him, let me play devil's advocate. You obviously like him. Why not play with him? You know the boundaries. You can protect yourself."

Could she? "What if he doesn't want to go that far?"

"Please. He can have any woman in the world, but he's here with you." Marley frowned. "Don't you want to kiss him again?"

"Yes," she said instantly, without thought.

"There you go."

"Excuse me," a voice said from behind her.

Nicole turned around.

The woman from Back to the Fuchsia stood

behind her with an armful of white tulips and a beleaguered expression. "I stopped by Romantic Notions to deliver these. It was closed, but then I saw you in the window, so like a creepy stalker I thought I'd accost you here."

"You're the sweetest stalker ever." Nicole took the bouquet. "There's no card."

"They're from your guy." The woman rolled her eyes. "Kooky celebrities."

She frowned at the flowers, knowing instantly who the florist meant. "Grif isn't my guy."

"Funny, since he wants flowers delivered to you every other day." She held her hand out. "Since you're just down the street, I'll deliver them myself, so I might as well introduce myself. Julie."

"Nicole, and I don't want flowers every other day."

"I know. Kooky celebrities." The woman gave her a crooked smile. "They have their own ideas. See you in a couple."

Nicole watched Julie leave. Then she turned around and stared at the flowers in her hand.

"You're going to need a whole bunch of vases," Marley said, sounding smug.

"It seems so."

"And a couple boxes of condoms, because no guy sends flowers to a girl he doesn't want."

She frowned at the tulips. They were her favorite.

"Just do it." Her friend sat back, looking eager. "You'll always wonder, and what do you have to lose?"

"I don't know. My heart?"

"No way. You're much too sensible to let it go that far."

Was she? She touched a flower petal and wondered if she'd passed sensible when she let Grif back into her life.

Half an hour later when she returned to Romantic Notions, the door was unlocked. Knowing she'd locked it, it could only mean Olivia, her boss and the owner, stopped by to check in. Eager, Nicole went inside.

Olivia stood at the counter, looking over the books, her baby boy squirming on her shoulder. Her hair was clipped back, a dark trail down her back. She wore dark jeans, a red top, and the most contented expression Nicole had ever seen. She looked up as the door chimed and smiled. "Nicole, you're a goddess."

"And I didn't even return with a latte for you." She hugged her boss, careful of the baby. "I didn't realize you were coming in today."

"Parker and I needed to get out of the house." She smiled softly at her son, running a hand over his head. "He's an adventurer, like his dad."

"May I?" She set the tulips on the counter and held out her hands.

"He's feeling especially rambunctious today," Olivia said as she passed him over. "He may spit on you, too."

Parker lunged at Nicole with a happy gurgle when she reached for him.

"Yikes." She caught him quickly, settling him on her hip.

"He moves a lot, but you won't drop him," Olivia said.

She hoped not. She bounced him a little, loving the delighted coo and the way his fingers caught her shirt and held on. She stroked his thatch of dark, downy hair and breathed in his baby scent, enchanted by the way he smiled at her. "I'm in love. He's adorable."

"I know. I tell Michael he's just like me." Olivia winked at her and then pointed to the books. "You're rocking the business. I think I should just take maternity leave forever and let you run the store."

She tried to imagine working there forever, but it didn't feel right. Sure, she'd been there the longest of any job, but forever was a long time. But to her boss, she just said, "I love working here."

"Let me put these in water for you and then we can go over the state of the union. I ordered a shipment of Chantelle that doesn't seem to have arrived yet." Olivia picked up the flowers and headed to the back. "And then you can tell me about your admirer."

"I don't have an admirer," she said quietly, not wanting to yell in Parker's ear.

She didn't think Olivia heard. Her boss came out of the back and set the vase of tulips next to a display of black satin Aubade and then immediately began quizzing her about what'd been going on since she'd been in a couple weeks ago. Nicole knew Olivia felt a little bit out of the loop, like she was abandoning her old baby for her new one, but Olivia managed to run things just as efficiently from home.

Nicole didn't mind. As far as she was concerned, she was happy to leave the business details to Olivia so she could do what she liked: sell romance.

"So." Olivia leaned her hip against the counter and crossed her arms. "Tell me about him."

She stilled, causing Parker to fuss. Patting his back, she rocked him back and forth. "I don't know what you're talking about."

"You're going to play dumb about all the flowers in here?"

"Yes."

"Then it's serious." Olivia pursed her lips. "You'll give notice if you decide to leave me, right?"

"I'm not leaving you." She rolled her eyes at Olivia's disbelieving gaze. "Seriously. I'm not going anywhere. It's not like that. He's just my old best friend from childhood who's visiting."

"Michael was my best friend from childhood, and he came back to stay."

"Yes, but Grif won't."

Olivia just stared at her.

"I mean it." She rubbed the baby's back, trying not to notice how nice he felt. "He needs a little help, and then he'll be on his way again. He doesn't stay in one place for long."

"Michael didn't either, until he came back and asked me to marry him."

Nicole stilled, caught by the vision of Grif on his knee, asking her to love him forever. Pathetic vision, because it wasn't ever going to happen. He was married to his guitar, whether he remembered it or not.

As if he sensed her unease, Parker began to fidget. She tried rocking him harder, but he began to mewl.

"He's hungry." Olivia held her arms out.

She reluctantly surrendered him to his mom, feeling the loss as soon as he was lifted from her. She'd never thought she'd want children, but maybe she did.

Olivia smiled down at her baby, serene love in her eyes. She rocked him back and forth as she pulled out a bottle from her diaper bag. He latched onto it eagerly, his long fingers curling around hers.

Nicole watched them, feeling their bond and being jealous.

"When Michael came back, I didn't want anything to do with him," Olivia said so softly that, for a moment, Nicole thought she was talking to her son. "I didn't think I could forgive him for leaving me. I didn't think he could make the commitment to settle down. But in the end, I had to try, and I'm glad I did, because otherwise I'd be missing the best days of my life."

Nicole swallowed thickly. "You're saying I should be open, because it'd be better to have loved and lost."

"Hell no." Olivia made a sour face. "Losing sucks. But if there's a window for happiness, you shouldn't miss climbing through it."

"Got it." She sighed. "I'll keep my windows open."

"He may come in through one."

She smiled ruefully. "And escape back out another."

Chapter Eleven

*T*HE —*SONS* WERE standing by the lockers, obviously waiting.

Rachel slowed down, wondering if she should just go on to French without her book or homework, but Madame Roche had been *un peu* peeved at her yesterday for not having her things with her. Madame had even threatened to call her dad. Rachel had wanted to tell her that wasn't much of a threat, because he didn't care what she did as long as it wasn't illegal.

But Madame Roche was nice, and Rachel felt bad for torturing her, so she actually did her homework last night. It'd been lame and easy, but whatever. No way was she going to take a zero for not doing it just because the —*sons* were waiting — presumably for her.

Sighing, she kept walking toward her locker. Maybe if she ignored them, they wouldn't exist. Or maybe her new underwear would give her magical powers to zap them away, or make her invisible.

But Madison stepped right in front of her, hands on her hips, glaring. "I know what you're doing."

Rachel looked at her locker, directly behind — *son* number one. "Getting my homework?"

Like a well-behaved sidekick, Addison backed up her friend with an equally vicious look. "FYI, you're not cute."

She rolled her eyes. "Can we cut with the obvious digs and just get to the point? I'm going to be late for French."

Madison poked her shoulder with a hard, skinny finger.

"*Ow.*" Rachel put her hand over the spot and glared at the girl. "What the hell?"

The girl walked up to her, so close Rachel could see the fine outline of her penciled brows. "Stay away from Aaron Hawke," she said, practically hissing. "You don't have anything he needs."

"And you know this... how?" Rachel stared at her steadily. "Because you and Aaron are BFFs?"

"I've known him way longer than you have. We've been in school together *forever*. We've talked about going out a bunch of times, but I wanted to wait."

It was on the tip of her tongue to tell the evil —*son* that Aaron *had* talked about her, but not in any sort of loving way. And if Aaron was so into Madison, why did he ask her over to dinner at his house?

But behind the malevolent light in the girl's gaze, there was hurt. As much as part of her wanted to exploit that, Rachel couldn't bring herself to pick at it and make it worse.

So she shrugged. "Whatever."

Both the ¬*sons* smirked as they got out of her way, but they still hung around as she opened her locker.

"I don't know what you were worried about, Mads," Addison said. "Aaron would never choose *her* over you. That's insane."

"I know. But it's better to have clear communication."

Rachel rolled her eyes again, knowing the girls couldn't see her since she faced her locker. She shut the door, clicked it locked, and stepped around the two witches. The final bell rang, and she sighed. Great—she was late.

"He could never like someone like her," Madison added. "I bet even her parents wish they didn't know her. I mean, her mom probably wishes she had a normal, pretty daughter."

"Yeah, I bet her mom totally regrets her."

Rachel stopped in her tracks. For a moment she just felt frozen, stunned that someone would talk about her mom.

Then the hurt set in. Would her mom want a better daughter? She didn't want to believe it, but she hadn't been acting her best lately.

Still, she knew her mom, and she knew her mom loved her no matter what. So she whirled around. "You don't know what you're talking about."

The —*sons* looked at her incredulously, like they couldn't believe she'd spoken to them. "Excuse me?" Madison said, flipping her hair over her shoulder.

"You know nothing about my family. You're just acting stupid and petty. Do you think Aaron's going to like that?"

Addison's jaw dropped as Madison strutted up to her, her mouth set in a mean line. "Don't even talk about him. I knew him first. Besides, I have way more going for me."

"Like what?" Rachel asked. "Community college?"

Addison gasped.

Madison got directly in her face. "You're just a loser that no one likes. I bet you don't even have a family. I bet your mom left you, because you were such a loser."

Her fury was quick and sharp. For a moment, Rachel knew she could strangle the evil —*son*.

Instead, she chose a different method of revenge. She lifted her chin and looked Madison in the eye. "If I were such a loser, Griffin Chase wouldn't be using my poem for lyrics for one of the songs on his upcoming release."

Both the —*sons* gasped, but it was Madison, of course, who spoke. "You're such a liar."

Her heart beat hard with the slight exaggeration. It wasn't an outright lie because she was going to make it come true. But she wasn't going to show weakness in front of the ⎯*sons of anarchy,* so she shrugged nonchalantly. "Believe it or not. It's the truth."

She turned on her heels and hurried to French. She was so late, but that was the least of her worries. She'd just told the mortal enemies that Griffin Chase was going to use her poem, and she hadn't managed to talk him into it yet.

What had she done?

Chapter Twelve

GRIF SAT ON his makeshift bed in Nicole's living room, Roddy's latest message playing in his head: *Chase, you're effin' blowing this. The execs are getting nervous.*

Well, so was he. He'd had a couple ideas but nothing of quality. His guitar mocked him from where it rested against the wall across the room.

The closed door of Nicole's room mocked him, too.

They'd hung out with Nicole's roommate that evening, and it'd been fun. Dinner at home, laughter and discussion. Susan had asked him about the rock star lifestyle, and he'd teased her about pushing drugs.

It's been nice. Really nice.

Nicole had been quiet, but she'd seemed to

have relaxed as the evening went on. At least he'd thought so until she announced she was retiring to her room.

He stared at the bedroom door. He was desperate to know what was going on in there. Was she drawing? Was she in bed? Did she have clothes on?

In high school, she'd gone through a phase when she fell asleep in her street clothes. She'd said then she didn't have to spend the extra minutes getting dressed for school. He couldn't see her sleeping in her clothes anymore. He saw her sleeping naked.

Not something he should be seeing. He squeezed his eyes shut, but the image burned bright even in the darkness of his mind. Sleek limbs, smooth skin, her shiny smile, and her dark hair fanning on her pillow.

He was lusting after his best friend.

It'd caught him by surprise. He hadn't expected it. He'd thought seeing her would be grounding, like it always had been. But there was nothing settling about seeing her. He felt off-kilter and confused.

He was dying for another kiss.

The problem was that he wasn't sure Nicole felt the same way, and pushing her too far could cost him the one person who meant as much to him as his family. He was torn between respecting her and getting her to take a chance.

A surge of desire made him stand up. One chance, one night. If he didn't try, he'd always wonder, and he didn't make it a habit to live with regrets. Before he could talk himself into sense, he strode to her door and opened it.

Startled, Nicole looked up from the book she was reading in bed.

Grif took her in: her mussed hair, her face innocent of makeup, the temptingly bare shoulders. He swallowed back the urge to crawl into bed with her and love her with his body. "What are you doing?"

"What are *you* doing?" Glaring, she pulled the sheets up to her neck. "You used to know how to knock."

Smiling, feeling alive for the first time in forever, he knocked on the wall. "Can Nicole come out to play?"

Nicole didn't look amused. She clutched her book in front of her chest. "It's late. I'm in bed, Grif."

"I see that." He wished he could see more. She had the covers pulled up so all that was showing was the thin straps of her top. Pink. He wondered if it was a nightgown, or just a top, and how much was covering the bottom. He tried not to imagine her wearing the underwear she'd drawn in her sketchpad.

Truthfully, since he'd seen her drawings, he'd had a hard time *not* imagining her in one of those creations. Especially that see-through black one.

He cleared his throat, shifting uncomfortably. "Let's go out."

"Out?" She blinked at him like he spoke a foreign language she didn't understand. "It's ten-thirty at night."

"Early still. Usually, I'm just getting going right about now."

"But I worked all day." She clutched her book closer to her chest, as if it were armor. "I'm tired."

He looked at the half-naked couple on the cover and read the title. *Never Love a Highlander*. He smiled. "You still read bodice rippers?"

She frowned indignantly at him. "They aren't bodice rippers. These are stories of love and hope."

"A physical book is so old school these days."

"I read digital books, too. Ebooks are convenient, but there's something to holding pages in your hand." She shrugged, and her strap fell off her shoulder.

It took all his willpower not to go to her and fix it. Or touch her skin. Or bury his face there and breathe her in.

He stepped back, in case his willpower failed. "Come on. Get dressed. The night is wasting."

"I'm tired, Grif," she repeated as though he were a child. "I was on my feet all day, and I just want to stay in bed and read."

It was on the tip of his tongue to invite himself between the sheets with her, but he bit his tongue and then played the guilt card. "Aren't you supposed to be helping me compose? Going out will help me."

She glared at him.

"The sooner I get it together, the sooner I'll be out of your hair," he pointed out, even though the thought didn't sit well with him.

"Fine." She shoved the covers aside.

And then he knew: shorts. Little frilly pink shorts that showed off her legs.

He stared at them, trying not to think about sliding his hands up her skin. In his mind they were smooth and soft and would wrap around his waist enthusiastically.

"Get out so I can get dressed," she said grumpily as she rooted on a chair through clothing piled on a chair in the corner.

"Want me to help?" he asked, not really kidding.

She threw a shirt at his head.

Catching it, he saluted and left the room, closing the door behind him. When it was shut tight, he lifted the shirt and inhaled. It smelled like her. It smelled delicious.

"Does she know?"

Startled, he looked up to find the curious gaze of Nicole's roommate on him.

Standing in the doorway of her bedroom, Susan nodded at the shirt. "Does she know you have a crush on her?"

It wasn't a crush. He didn't know what it

was — lust or love, nostalgia or forever — but whatever it was, it was stronger than a crush. "No."

"Don't tell her."

He blinked. "Excuse me?"

She gestured him closer, waiting to whisper, "Nicole flits from thing to thing. Men are no different. She loses interest in them faster than she grows tired of her fancy underwear."

"What are you saying?"

"I don't know." Susan smiled wide. "I just like you. I'd have thought you'd be a big phony, but I think you might be good for her. She's one in a million. You understand what I'm saying?"

"I think so," he said even though he wasn't sure.

He was rewarded with a brilliant smile. "Good," she said, patting his chest. "Have fun tonight."

She retreated into her room.

Nicole's door opened. She looked hot in tight jeans, dark red boots, and a sweater. Her hair was pulled into a ponytail, and she'd put on a little lipstick — not that it covered the surly downturn on her mouth.

"You look eager," he joked. He tipped his head toward the door. "Come on. I promise it'll be fun."

She slipped into her jacket, grumbling under her breath. Then she said, "Did I hear you and Susan talking?"

"Yeah." He grabbed a cap and his coat before escorting her out of the apartment. "She's a nice girl."

"Where's your car?" Nicole asked when she saw the town car waiting at the curb.

"Parked." He opened the door for her and gave the driver the club's name. "I thought it'd be better, in case we decided to drink."

"Responsible of you. Where are we going?"

"A little club. A friend of mine is playing there tonight."

"You have friends?" she asked as she slid into the car.

"Trey's not picky."

Nicole curled onto the back seat, looking around with wide eyes. "I've never been in a limo."

"It's just a town car."

"In my world, it's a limo." She ran a hand over the leather seats. "You must be used to this though."

He shook his head. "We travel in a bus most of the time. It's a luxury bus, but nothing is luxurious when you have six unshaven guys around you twenty-four/seven."

She faced him. "And when you're home?"

"My parents' house?"

"Is that what you consider home?"

"It's more home than my apartment in L.A." He smiled ruefully. "I'm at my apartment so rarely that I have a hard time finding the bottle opener."

Nicole frowned at him. "That's sad."

"It's certainly pathetic." It wore on him, especially since he'd become less than enchanted with music.

They arrived at the club. He got out and held his hand out for Nic.

She stared at it too long before she put her palm in his. Her grip felt hesitant and he hated that, so he held her hand firm and sure. When she looked at him askance, he said, "The neighborhood is sketchy. I'm protecting you."

She rolled her eyes. "It's the Tenderloin, not Libya. I think I'll be fine."

"Is holding my hand so awkward?" he asked as they walked into the bar.

"Yes." She faced him, but she didn't withdraw her hand. "Are you saying it's not?"

"It's different." He held their entwined hands between them, looking down at her fingers wrapped in his. Yes, it felt strange, but new-strange rather than bad-strange. It was like trying on a pair of new boots—they felt a little stiff but you knew they'd be your favorite pair soon. "But you have to admit that it feels nice."

"I don't have to admit anything."

He grinned. "You're in a mood. Come on. I know what'll help."

He dragged her to an empty bar stool and seated her on top. He pulled his cap lower over his forehead and caught the bartender's attention. He ordered two beers and then impulsively requested two shots of whiskey as well.

Nicole raised her brows as the bartender slipped the shots across the counter. "I'm not partying hard tonight," she said as she lifted it.

"One shot, to warm us up." He lifted his glass.

She touched it to his and tossed it back, grimacing and taking a sip of her beer. "We've never had drinks together, much less shots."

"That's not true." He set the glass down. "Remember the time we raided your parents' liquor cabinet?"

"Of all the liquor, we picked Chartreuse because of the neon green color." She laughed. "I still think Chartreuse is disgusting. Why did my parents even stock it?"

He loved the sound of her laughter. He'd sample it into a song, only he wanted it all to himself. "It was a blessing that we hated the taste. Think of the hangover it'd have caused."

"The band is good." She turned around so her back was to the bar and beat her hand against her thigh in rhythm to the music. "The lead isn't bad. His voice isn't as good as yours, but he can play the guitar."

"You think my voice is good?"

She made a face at him. "Don't fish. You know I've always believed in you and your talent."

He wanted to take her hand again. He wanted ed to confess everything that was filling his heart right in that moment. He wanted to tell her he'd been a fool to leave her for so long, and that her absence had left a big gaping hole in his world.

"A good friend of mine is in the audience tonight," a voice cut over the music. "Maybe he'll come up and play with us?"

Grif looked up to see Trey looking at him questioningly.

Nicole nudged him. "Go. It's what we're here for."

No, tonight was about being with Nicole. But the way she looked at him, like she wanted him so desperately to sing, got to him. He nodded, taking his cap off and running a hand over his hair.

There was a collective shocked gasp from the crowd, and then Trey announced, "Give it up for Griffin Chase."

A rousing round of applause filled the room, but he only saw Nicole's pleased smile. He kissed her cheek, unable to help it, and then joined the band on stage, accepting the guitar Trey handed him.

He took the instrument respectfully, giving it the due it deserved. He slipped the strap over his head, took a moment to tune it, and then smiled at the audience.

They smiled back, excited and eager.

Something in his chest shifted. He truly did love seeing the happiness in the faces when they listened to him.

Then he looked at Nicole.

She sat on the edge of her seat, her beautiful eyes wide and full of belief in him. She smiled and nodded in encouragement.

He returned his attention to the crowd, his fingers strumming idly, getting the feel of the guitar. "I wrote this song for my best friend a long time ago," he said, launching into *Lost*.

The band took a second and then jumped in, playing along expertly. He sang the words directly to Nicole, seeing the shock in her eyes. The song ended, and they launched right into the Beatles, followed by the Rolling Stones.

He winked at Trey and lifted the guitar strap over his head. Trey leaned into the microphone and said, "Griffin Chase, everybody."

The applause was loud. Waving his thanks, Grif headed back to Nicole. The band began singing their next song as he made his way through the crowd. He paused to acknowledge fans, but he only had eyes for her.

When he finally reached her, he held out his hand. "Dance with me."

For a second, he didn't think she was going to accept his invitation, but then she put her hand in his and slid off the stool. He led her to the dance floor and whirled her into his arms.

She nestled into him, raising her mouth to whisper in his ear. "Were you serious? You wrote that song for me?"

He touched the corner of her mouth, trying hard to resist kissing her. "It was my first big hit. I was playing with some band that broke up years ago, and I was homesick, and I missed you. The song came to me in a wave. You've always been my inspiration, Nicole."

They swayed slowly to the music. At first, she didn't say anything, but then she said, "You still have the arrowhead."

"I never take it off."

Her lips pursed into a frown. "You don't have to say things like that just to score points."

"I'm not." He gazed into her eyes so she could see the truth in his.

She rested her head against his shoulder. "We can't do this."

"Why not?"

"You're going to leave."

"I'm here with you now. Besides, won't it be better that way? You don't like to be trapped by any one thing. This is good for both of us. You don't have to worry about me wanting more."

"And you?"

He got to love her, even if it was for entirely too short. He pulled her close, so there was no question that he was aroused. "What do you think?"

She gazed at him. He slowed down their dance, pulling her flush against him. She wrapped her arms around his neck, shimmying sexily against him.

He ran his hand up her side, resting just below the swell of her breasts. His grip tightened of its own volition.

She licked her lips, lifting her face. It was the most natural thing in the world to lower his mouth to hers and kiss her.

Chapter Thirteen

NICOLE SAW THE kiss coming and did nothing to stop it.

She didn't want to.

She didn't want to think about it either. She closed her eyes and just felt.

It felt wonderful.

They stopped swaying to the music despite the people gyrating around them, bumping into them. The noise of the room faded until the only thing she heard was the beat of her heart heavy in her head. Nothing else existed—just Grif and the touch of his lips.

His arm snaked around her waist, anchoring her to him, while his other hand cupped her face, his fingers trailing over her as if he was trying to memorize her.

She pressed herself closer, feeling him hard and insistent between them.

She'd dreamt of kissing him again. She'd spent hours thinking about it, imagining it—praying for it, if she were being honest.

The reality of the kiss now was nothing like she'd imagined.

His fingers slipped into her hair, massaging the base of her skull so she felt like purring. She pressed closer—she needed to be closer.

He kissed across her cheek, to her jaw, and then whispered in her ear. "Unless you want to be on the front page of *People Magazine* tomorrow we should take this party someplace more private."

More private. She shivered, knowing what he was suggesting, knowing he was asking for her consent. "And then what?" she said.

He gazed at her soberly. "Whatever you want, Nicole."

That was the problem: she wasn't sure what she wanted, though at the moment she was pretty sure it involved more of his talented mouth on various parts of her body.

Grif rubbed his thumb along her jaw. "Doubts?"

He knew her too well. "Yes."

"We're not eighteen, Nic." He brushed her hair aside. "We're going into this with our eyes open, right?"

Her eyes may be wide open, but she wasn't sure what she was seeing. "We're crossing a dangerous line, and we won't be able to go back. What if sex sucks?"

Smiling slowly, he touched the corner of her mouth. "If our kisses are any indication, sex might kill us but it definitely won't suck."

"True." She nodded. "Get me out of here."

"Let's go."

The car was waiting for them outside. The driver hopped out to open the door for them, and they slid in.

Grif turned to her. "Where should we go?"

She almost said her place, because they were both staying there after all, but then she thought about the logistics. Susan was there, and did she really want a strange man in her bed?

Well, granted, it was Grif, not a strange man.

But she'd never brought any man home. She'd never had sex with anyone in her bed, not even the guys she dated. It seemed so personal and, frankly, she never stuck with them for very long. So she said, "Hotel."

He didn't bat a lash. "Which one?"

Was it odd that he didn't question her choice? "Any hotel. Pick one."

He pulled out his phone. In a few seconds, he motioned to the driver. "The Four Seasons."

It was only a few blocks away, on Market Street, so they were there in minutes. She looked out at the subtle placard on the hotel's entrance as a doorman opened her door for them. Fancy. She shrugged. If you were going to have an affair, why not the Four Seasons?

Grif took her hand and led her inside. Nicole knew she should have felt mortified at checking in at a hotel—a really nice hotel—after midnight, with a well-recognized celebrity no less. But she was more excited than anything. This was romantic in a big way. No guy had ever done this for her.

No guy had ever treated her the way Grif did. Flowers. Singing to her. Kissing her so amazingly.

Yes, she knew he wanted something from her, but he knew he had her help. Bribery wasn't necessary.

Except she knew deep down in her heart, he wasn't trying to bribe her. Griffin Chase didn't need to resort to bribery. He'd never done anything he hadn't felt compelled to do.

Slipping his sunglasses on and making sure his cap was firmly on his head, Grif stopped at the front desk and smiled at the woman sitting there. "I'd like to check into a room, please."

The woman melted under his smile, of course, although based on the fact that she hadn't started drooling, she obviously hadn't see beyond his disguise. "Do you have a reservation, Mr...?"

"Gallagher. Roddy Gallagher." He pulled out an American Express card out of his wallet.

As he handed it over, Nicole glanced at the name. Sure enough, it had the fake name Grif used. She arched her brows at him.

He squeezed her hand and focused his charm on the woman.

Who batted her eyes shamelessly. "Thank you, Mr. Gallagher. For how many nights?"

"One night," he replied as though he showed up in hotels after midnight with a woman in tow all the time.

Nicole didn't like that thought.

Was this a bad idea? Maybe she shouldn't be there.

But even as she had the thought, she knew there was no question that she was going to go through with this. She wasn't promiscuous, always taking care in picking who she ended up with, and this was happening way faster than normal. But it felt inevitable. Right.

And, if she were honest, she *really* wanted Grif.

Thanking the receptionist, he turned to Nicole. "Ready?"

Any more ready, and she'd be naked right there in the lobby. But to reassure herself that she was doing the right thing, she got up on her tiptoes and kissed him.

The contact zapped her even though she'd meant it to be light. *This* was why they were in the Four Seasons, taking such a big chance with their friendship. This crazy electric thing between them.

He hummed, his hand gripping her hair. "It's not too late to back out."

She thought about the kiss and remembered being draped across his body early that one morning. She'd be out of her mind to back down now. Marley would never forgive her.

So she did the only logical thing: she pressed herself against him and kissed him again with all the nervous eagerness in her body.

He groaned with a hunger that excited her, catching her up in his arms. "It's going to be great, Nic," he murmured against her mouth.

Yes. Nodding, she led him to the elevator.

When they reached their floor, instead of leading her to their room, he surprised her by lifting her into his arms and carrying her. Without releasing her, he opened the door and headed straight to the bed, lowering her and following directly on top of her.

She sighed, loving the weight of his body on her. She tugged his shirt up and touched his naked back, hooking her legs in the crook of his knees to keep him close.

Leaning on one arm, he pushed up all her layers—coat and shirt—until his hand cupped her breast over her bra. His fingers teased her nipple to standing through the thin lace, rolling and massaging until she was writhing under him.

"Grif," she gasped, trying to get closer to him.

"Yes?" He nibbled on her collarbone.

"I need more."

"I can give you more." He sat up, undid her pants, and pulled them and her underwear down. Then he dumped condoms out from his pocket and unbuttoned his jeans.

She stared at the condoms littering the bed. "Planning ahead?"

"It's called hope." He pulled his erection out and covered it in one of the rubbers.

Nicole wanted to tell him she had a clean bill of health and was on the pill, but maybe this was better. It was a symbolic barrier—a reminder not to get *too* close.

Grif worked her coat and top off and then slid his finger under the strap of her exposed bra. "I'm torn between asking you to model this for me and tearing it off you."

"That's a dilemma."

"I'm not sure I can last through a show. Can I get a rain-check? For next time?"

"There's going to be a next time?"

"I know I'm jumping the gun, but based on the events so far, I'm willing to bet that we'll want a next time. Maybe you'll even model something you've designed yourself."

She stilled. "What?"

He had the grace to look abashed. "I may have snooped. But before you get bent out of shape, your lingerie designs are incredible. I especially like the sheer black one."

"You weren't supposed to look," she said weakly as she blushed. She'd designed that black one with him in mind.

"I know, but I'm happy I did. It gives me something to look forward to for the next time."

His praise caused a rush of delight followed immediately by uneasiness. She hid her feelings behind a sassy smile and ran her hands along his chest. "Bold, making promises for the next time when you haven't delivered this time."

"Are you worried I won't deliver?"

Arching up, she said, "Well, you *have* been all talk so far."

"And I'm not meeting your needs. I'll have to rectify that." He lowered his head and kissed her.

Blazing hot, it stole her breath. She arched up into it, giving him space to reach around her to unhook her bra. He swept it away and, kissing his way down the center of her body, to take the tips of her breasts in his mouth, one at a time, before working his way down.

Before she could catch her breath, he pressed his next kiss right between her legs.

She gasped in surprise, and then he licked into her and she gasped in pleasure. She gripped his hair as he did it again — and again. Her head swam, and she gripped the bed covers to anchor herself.

He loved her with his mouth, like he couldn't get enough of her. Like she was the most delicious chocolate dessert and he wanted to lap up every last bite.

Out of nowhere, her climax hit her, making her shout out, her thighs tensing around his head. She was about to tell him to stop when he slid back up and pushed into her.

He gazed into her eyes, brushing her hair out of her eyes. Then he smiled, kissed her, and she felt so right.

He rolled his hips into her, and sharp jabs of electric shock zipped through her. She gasped, grabbing his arms, about to tell him it was too intense, that she was going to die, when she suddenly came again.

He slowed down, long, hard strokes deep inside her, the column of his neck taut. He thrust into her one more time, tensing, crying out her name as he came, too.

Instead of crushing her with his weight, he rolled onto his back, pulling her over him.

She began to sit up, to get off, but he held her in place. Feeling him stir inside her, she looked at him, a flare of desire miraculously lighting her up all over again. "Again?"

"Yes." He pulled her on top, urging her to ride him.

"I need your cowboy hat," she said, propping herself up.

His fingers tightened on her and he pulsed inside her, obviously liking the thought. "That can be arranged."

"Is there anything you can't arrange?"

"For you?" He shook his head, his smile sweet. "Even the moon, Nicole."

Her heart flopped, but she shook it off. Tonight was only about pleasure—about Happily Right Now. Happily Ever After didn't happen with a man like Griffin Chase, no matter how much you wanted it.

Chapter Fourteen

In the Regencies Nicole loved, the heroines were always limp with satisfaction at the end of lovemaking, but she herself had never experienced that sort of ultimate pleasure. Not that she didn't like sex — she loved it. It was always good — or at least passable enough.

Sex with Grif was beyond anything she'd ever imagined. She'd *screamed*.

It'd been magical.

Except for the one part where he'd confessed about looking at her sketchpad. There wasn't anything she could do about it now, but it didn't mean she felt any less exposed. Except it was Grif, and he knew her better than almost anyone.

And he knew her much better now, having explored her body all night long.

Apparently she'd slept tangled in him, his legs scissored between hers, his arm draped around her, her head nestled into his shoulder. She liked it, probably more than she should. It felt good, weighty as opposed to light and insubstantial, and that worried her. It was supposed to be easy.

Actually it was incredibly easy.

She cuddled into him, and he stirred, nuzzling her shoulder. "What time do you have to be at work?" he asked, his voice husky with sleep.

She'd forgotten about reality. She wilted, wishing she could stay here forever. "At eleven."

Grif craned his neck to look at the clock on the bedside stand. "I don't think I've ever been so glad it's only nine o'clock."

She chuckled. "You never liked to wake up early in school either."

"I'm civilized." He rolled on top of her. "You'll like to stay in bed, too."

When she felt his hardness, she sighed happily. "Maybe."

"Maybe?" He lifted his head, as though scenting a challenge. "Maybe? Am I going to have to prove it?"

She sighed again as his erection touched her intimately. "I'm not sure I'll believe you until you do."

"In that case..." He scratched her neck with his raspy cheek, his hand stealing down between their bodies, all the way down to where she needed him most.

She arched up, sensitive from the night's play, and then gasped in pleasure as his fingers homed in on the perfect spot.

He lowered his head to her breast, teasing her nipple with his tongue. "We need to order room service," he murmured against her skin.

"We do?" She speared her fingers in his hair. She could care less about food, not when he was snacking on her.

"You can't go to work hungry. And you need to shower too."

She kissed down the column of his neck. "I suppose you're offering to wash my back."

"Definitely." He stood up and scooped her in his arms.

"Wait." She pointed at the bed. "We only just started."

"I know." He kissed her forehead, and then her neck. "We'll finish in the shower."

Her heart skipped with anticipation, and all she could do was nod in consent, and, later, scream some more.

They never did order room service.

Grif helped her shower and get dressed, the whole time wishing he could undress her again. He leaned against the sink as she smoothed her hair in a ponytail.

She grimaced at her reflection. "That's the best I can do."

Any better and he wasn't sure he'd be able to let her go. Despite the fact that she had nothing more than a little gloss on her lips, she was luminous. This morning her eyes sparkled with more than their usual light. The one flaw was a patch of redness that marked her neck, where his stubble had abraded her, but he even liked that. He liked knowing she wore his brand.

KT would call him pathetic.

"Next time I'll bring makeup with me," Nicole

said with one last look in the mirror. She faced him. "You know, I can take a cab to work if you want to stay here longer."

"I'll take you." He kissed her glistening lips. "And later we can discuss next time."

Her eyes widened. "I didn't mean—"

"I want it, too, Nic," he assured her.

She swallowed audibly and then nodded. When she spoke, her voice was a little hoarse. "We should go."

He put his cap and sunglasses on and took her hand. "Come then."

They walked down, hand in hand. The doorman hailed them a taxi.

The cab ride was silent. He was about to ask Nicole what was going through her head when a faint strain of a melody rose in his mind. He stilled, listening, knowing from experience that it had to work itself to the surface. Forcing it would only make it more elusive. So he held onto Nicole's hand and hoped it wasn't just a fleeting hallucination.

When they arrived she faced him. "Grif—"

Before she could finish whatever she'd been

about to say, he kissed her. And then because it was delicious, he kissed her again, lingering, feeling his chest fill with desire and longing that had to do with more than just sex.

Nicole melted against him, sighing, just like he'd intended. He lifted her chin. "See you after work?"

"Yes." She smiled at him and slid out of the car. She waved and headed to open the store.

He watched her and then turned to tell the taxi driver their address. But he noticed Grounds for Thought across the street, so he paid the cabbie and went to get a cup of coffee.

Putting in an order for coffee and a scone, he managed to make it to a seat in the back without a scene or anyone recognizing him. He left his hat and sunglasses on, wanting privacy.

Wanting space to think about Nicole.

It was going to be a long day without her. He wished she were sitting there with him.

Here with you.

He pulled out the notepad she'd given him and flipped to a blank page.

Here with you. He wrote the words down, humming a measure of that tune playing in his head.

The barista delivered his coffee, but he hardly noticed. More images came to him: Nicole's hair, messy on his pillow; the slide of her leg, smooth against his; her smile, adorably crooked, so slow in the night. He wrote them all down, not sure how they fit together or even if they would.

His heart beat heavily, excited, feeling a surge of creativity he hadn't experienced in so long. He was afraid to focus on it too closely—what if it vanished?

But he had a feeling it was only just reappearing, and that it'd be stronger than ever.

Because of Nicole.

Chapter Fifteen

*I*T WAS COLD, and sitting on the cold concrete curb wasn't helping matters. Rachel huddled in her jacket, hating the wind. It felt like winter in San Francisco even though it was spring.

A shadow fell over her.

Glancing up, she saw Aaron looming over her like a giant. The instant happiness she felt surprised her.

"Hey," he said.

Rachel wanted to tell him to go away but she couldn't make herself say the words. She heard the paper she was waiting to give Griffin Chase crinkle in her hand, and she forced her grip to relax.

Aaron took her silence as an invitation and sat down next to her. "What's going on?"

"What makes you think something's going on?"

He pointedly looked at her head.

Her hand went to the ski cap she's put on because she'd been so cold. "I'm just trying out a new look."

He grinned. "It's working for you."

The door to Romantic Notions opened. Rachel sat up, alert, but it was only an older woman who walked out. She slumped back down. Where was he? Had she missed him? Maybe he'd gone back to Los Angeles or wherever.

He couldn't be gone. The *–sons* would torture her for the rest of her life if she didn't get Griffin Chase to make her poem into a song.

"You must have a major thing for underwear," Aaron said, pulling her out of her thoughts.

She glanced at him. "Why do you say that?"

"Because it's like you're casing the joint. Are you planning a heist?"

"Of course not."

He grinned. "I love it when you get prissy."

"I'm not prissy," she said, hearing the prissiness in her voice.

"So why are we sitting here?"

"*I'm* sitting here because I'm waiting. *You're* sitting here to plague me."

He didn't take the hint, simply asking, "What are you waiting for?"

She couldn't say she was waiting for Griffin Chase. Then she'd have to say why, and she wasn't ready to confess that much to a boy she barely knew, even if he was cute and funny and smart. So she said, "Nothing."

"Then come have a drink with me."

"I can't."

"Come on. Grounds for Thought has awesome chocolate chip cookies, and they bake a batch to be ready specially after school."

"I—"

"We still haven't gotten together to talk about my term paper. You promised you'd help."

She hadn't, but she figured it wasn't the time to point that out. "I'd be risking my life if I had a drink with you."

"Your life?" His brow furrowed.

"Madison told me she'd gut me if I didn't stay away from you."

"Isn't that reason enough to come eat cookies with me?"

She looked at Romantic Notions. She could keep an eye on the door from inside the coffee shop and rush out if Griffin Chase showed up. "You're right. Let's go. But we sit in the front."

Aaron stood up. "If only I'd known Madison was the way to your heart sooner."

"If you're going to be caustic, I'll stay here."

"Caustic?" He grinned and hiked his bag and hers onto his shoulder. "I love how you talk."

"I don't talk in any way," she mumbled as she got up and dusted off her butt.

"I noticed it the first time I saw you. You walked into class your first day late, and Michael pointed to the clock and asked if you were lost, and you replied 'No, just temporally challenged.'"

"You heard me?" She thought she'd said it quietly.

"Yeah." He laughed as he held the door open for her. "It cracked me up."

She walked by him, feeling her face go red as she brushed the front of his jacket. She hurried inside to a table in the front. It wasn't exactly by the window, but from the chair on the right she had a good enough view.

Aaron walked up and set their bags next to the table. "What would you like?"

"I can get it," she murmured, reaching for her bag. Her dad always gave her wads of money. As if money made up for the fact that he was never around.

"It's my treat." Aaron put his hand on top of hers.

She froze, looking down at where he touched her. His hand was warm and big, making her feel small and delicate. She felt a funny tingle in the pit of her stomach, and she looked up, startled.

Smiling, he withdrew his hand. "Mocha?"

"Hot chocolate," she replied, rubbing the back of her hand on her jeans to get rid of the tingly feeling.

"Be right back."

Sitting down, she watched him stride to the counter. The blonde was there, and he greeted her by name.

His smile was so nice. *He* was nice. She wasn't sure why he was being nice to her. She wanted to resist it, but she liked it. She'd never been into the boys at her school in Manhattan, because whenever she looked at them she remembered when they were six years old and lame. Her mom had always said she'd know when a boy was right for her.

Was Aaron right?

Rachel had no idea. She wished her mom were here so she could ask.

He came back with a plate of cookies. "I didn't know what you'd like, so I got a bunch to share."

"Why do you hang out with me so much?" she heard herself blurt out.

He blinked at her, like the question surprised him. "Because I like you."

"You don't know me."

"I know you like snickerdoodles."

She looked down at the cookie in her hand. "I like cinnamon."

"I know you live with your dad, and that you're sad about your mom," he continued. "I know you're witty and are a writer, even if you don't write much."

"How do you know that?" she asked with a frown.

"You have that red diary, but it's all blank."

The notebook her mom gave her. She swallowed. "You noticed that?"

He shrugged as he snagged a chocolate chip cookie for himself. "It's hard not to notice."

The blonde brought their drinks, smiling at them. She was pretty, but it was the happiness in her eyes that caught Rachel's attention. "Here you go," she said, setting them on the table. "Let me know if you need anything more."

She watched the lady walk away, knowing Aaron was studying *her*. She avoided eye contact for as long as she could, and then scowled at him. "I'm not really interesting."

"I think you are." He pushed her hot chocolate toward her. "What do you like to write?"

She shrugged, dipping a finger in the whipped cream and licking it. When she realized he was still staring at her. She hated that her face flushed. She hated that she liked him staring at her.

"Are you going to leave me hanging?" he prompted her. "You know I'm going to imagine you write limericks or something."

"Limericks?" She raised her eyebrows.

"There once was a girl from New York. She thought she was a total dork—"

"I'm not a dork!" she protested. "And I don't write limericks. I write stories and poems."

"A-ha!" He held a finger in the air. "The way to get you to answer is to insult you. Your hair is…"

She waited for him to finish, and when he didn't, she frowned. "Is my hair that bad?"

"It's actually really pretty," he admitted sheepishly. "I couldn't come up with anything bad to say about it."

Something inside her softened, and before she could think about it, she said, "I don't write very much anymore."

"Because of your mom?"

She nodded, startled that he'd guess it. "Sh— she used to buy me notebooks and encourage me to write. She was a freelance editor. She loved books. *Loved* them. One time my parents had a fight because she went to bed to read in the afternoon, because she wanted to crawl into bed with the hero."

"It must have been a hot book."

"I think it was a historical." She smiled a little,

remembering her mother describe the book, so excited to get back to it. "She used to tell me that books stay with people and become their best friends, even after the person was gone."

"Do you want to be a writer?"

She shrugged. "I haven't thought of it much."

"I don't believe that."

"What do you want to be?" she asked, wanting to turn the tables on him but also curious. Okay — mostly curious.

"If I could be anything, I'd play pro golf. I like soccer a lot, but I only play it because we don't have a golf league in school."

"Seriously?" Rachel bit her lip to keep from grinning.

"What's wrong with that?"

"Nothing." She didn't really know anything about it, except that it was boring and you wore plaid. "And if you don't make the pro golf team?"

"Circuit," he corrected. "Then I'd like to be a research scientist."

She pretended to gag.

He laughed. "Well, it's a hundred times better than being a writer. "

"No, it's not." She leaned forward. "When you're a writer, you can be anything for a little while. A golfer, a scientist, a pretty girl, a millionaire, or a rock star. You could try something new each day."

"I get it." He nodded. "So if it's so satisfying, why don't I ever see you writing? Your diary is blank."

She gulped without taking a sip of her hot chocolate, afraid she'd choke. "My mom got that notebook for me. I don't want to write in it."

He didn't say anything.

She told herself she didn't care if he did or not, because there was no way he'd understand. If she filled it up, she wouldn't have anything left of her mother's.

Aaron said very softly, "I didn't know her, but I bet she'd have wanted you to use it."

Then he surprised her by adding, "Maybe sometime you'll let me read something you wrote."

No way. Never. Just the thought of it made her gut cramp.

But then she saw her mom's gentle smile, always encouraging her. So she swallowed and shrugged noncommittally.

"I'll take that." He grinned at her and picked up another cookie.

On her walk home, Rachel realized she'd forgotten all about Griffin Chase.

Letting herself into the house, she told herself it was okay. He probably hadn't been there anyway, and hanging out with Aaron had been nice.

As she locked the door, she heard a sound in the kitchen. Confused, wondering if the housekeeper was still there, she went to check it out.

It was her dad, drinking a glass of the vile green juice he'd started drinking since they moved here. He was scrolling through his phone, probably checking email. He was always working.

He glanced up when she walked in and smiled. "Hi, sweetheart."

She felt a pang of jealousy at the contentedness on his face. Why was she the only one who felt miserable? She mumbled something as she opened the refrigerator and got out a bottle of water.

"I made reservations out for dinner."

Frowning, she turned around. "Why?"

"Because they supposedly have a lobster mac and cheese to die for, and I know how much you love that."

"I loved mom's lobster mac and cheese." She wanted to take back the surly words the second her dad's happy expression melted.

"You should give it a try, Rachel," he suggested gently. "You might like this, too. There's no reason to deprive yourself of something you love just because your mom is gone. She wouldn't expect you to just stop enjoying life."

Except that it felt wrong to enjoy anything when her mom was dead. A surge of anger boiled in her chest, and she glared at her dad. "I know you haven't."

He sighed. "Rachel, I just want you to be happy."

"Then leave me alone," she murmured, stomping all the way to her bedroom. She closed the door and went directly to her laptop. Dropping her head on her desk, she exhaled. Then she sat up and began to type.

To: wendy.rosenbaum@gmail.com
From: rachel_rose@gmail.com
Subject: Life sucks.

Dad is acting WEIRD.

Tonight he wanted to take me to get lobster mac and cheese. You know I only like yours. What's he trying to do? And does he seem happy?

Also (and not related to the previous issue) there's this boy. His name is Aaron, and he's really nice. He gets me in a way no one else has, not even Dad. Except you, but you're gone.

How do I know if I like him?

I don't have anyone to ask. Dad wouldn't understand. I'm not sure Dad even knows who I am anymore.

What should I do? I think I like him. It doesn't seem fair to like him though. I shouldn't be happy, not when you're gone.

Chapter Sixteen

LYRICS AND CHORDS had been echoing in his head the entire week — since the morning he'd woken up with Nicole at the Four Seasons.

He paced in KT's sound studio, hands in his pockets. Fortunately, his friend sat at her piano, focused on a song she was writing for her sister and not paying attention to his mania.

It was driving him crazy — that one strain of a melody, over and over. Sweet and soft, with the potential for an edge. Just like Nicole. Elusive, also like Nicole.

Their relationship had consisted of furtive hook-ups whenever they got a moment alone. The illicit lovemaking, hidden from Susan's attentive eye, made him feel like a teenager. He told himself it was hot and exciting, but the truth was he wanted the intimacy of sleeping with Nicole at night, too. Maybe if he could hold Nicole, he might be able to pin down the damn music in his head.

Setting his notepad on the closed lid of KT's grand piano, he picked up one of the guitars she kept in the corner, sat on a stool, and began to play the tune. He hummed a little with it, feeling lyrics on the tip of his tongue. *Here with you now…*

"If it were me," KT said suddenly, "I'd do this with the music."

Pausing, he listened as she turned his few measures into a complicated melody.

Something in his head clicked, and there it was. A stir of excitement in his chest, he started playing along, layering haunting mystery on top of her music.

This was it. It felt *right*. He pulled out his phone to record what they were playing.

KT nodded when he joined back in. Then she played a section over and said, "I'd repeat this part as the refrain."

"Yes." He set the guitar down and got up to jot down notes in the notebook Nicole had given him.

He noted the melody, writing down the complicated twist KT gave his original tune. He wrote down the lyrics, and then a few more lines that flowed with the rest.

KT craned her neck to look at his notebook. "Are those drawings part of the song?"

"Nicole gave me this book and told me to fill it with my thoughts."

"So you've been thinking a lot about stick figures with daggers in their hearts?"

He shrugged. "It's the only thing I can draw."

KT tipped her head and stared at him. "What's going on between you and Nicole?"

Amazing, amazing lovemaking. "Not what you're insinuating."

"Bullshit." KT arched her brow. "My ear is trained to hear subtle differences, and when you said her name, your tone changed."

He picked up the guitar and strummed the melody again, to drown her out.

"You can ignore me all you want, but I know what's going on," she said. "I recognize loving afterglow when I see it. Sex by itself is just messy."

"Only if you do it right, darlin'." He winked at her.

KT rolled her eyes. "Just be careful. Being a musician and having a relationship don't mix unless you're both on the same path."

He knew that. He'd seen too many couples fall apart—badly—to think that he could have a regular relationship alongside his career in its current incarnation. Hell—he'd tried it himself, but it'd become apparent really quickly that it wasn't going to work. "Nic was very clear about not wanting a relationship."

"All women want relationships."

"You don't."

His friend shrugged. "I'm the exception that proves the rule."

He kissed her forehead. "You're a nut, but you're cute, so at least you have that going for you."

KT pointed to the door. "Get out. I'm done with you."

Grinning, he returned the guitar to its stand. "Thanks for brainstorming my song with me."

"I expect to be credited." She ran her nimble fingers over the keyboard in a hard melody, but the corner of her mouth kicked up.

He tucked the notepad in his coat and tapped the top of the grand piano. "See ya."

She nodded, already immersed in her song.

He checked the time as he started to walk back to Nicole's apartment. She should be home from work by now.

The past few days had been strange. Not bad—just strange. He hadn't known what to expect, but the passion hadn't cooled. But it wasn't just sex either. Last night, they'd ended up having a nice dinner at home with Susan followed by a wicked game of Scrabble. Nicole, of course, lost interest halfway into the game, but Susan had managed to rally her to hang in there until the end.

Susan was a nice girl. He wasn't the least bit intrigued by her.

Nicole, on the other hand, fascinated him in a way he'd never experienced. It baffled him—he knew her already. He'd known her forever—there shouldn't have been any mystery left there.

But there was.

His phone rang. Thinking it might be Nicole, he pulled it out, wincing when he saw it was his manager again. He let it go and then listened to the voicemail.

"Grif, what the fu—eff are you doing in San Francisco? I saw the hotel charge on my American Express card, not to mention the pictures posted all over Facebook and Twitter of you dancing with that girl. *This* is how you work on your new music? The studio execs are *not* happy." There was a pause, then he added, "Call me. And please tell me you're using condoms. Paternity suits are a bitch."

Shaking his head, Grif tucked the phone away and walked up the steps to Nicole's apartment. The light was on inside, and his heart hammered with hope that it was her. Alone. He was dying to take her in his arms.

Nicole was already home, standing at the counter in the kitchen, reading a book as something warmed in the microwave. She looked up as he walked in.

His breath caught, the way it seemed to whenever he looked into her eyes. Given the choice between another hit album and Nicole, he knew exactly which one he'd choose, and Roddy wouldn't be psyched about his answer.

Grif took his hat and sunglasses off, setting them on the kitchen table. "Is Susan home yet?"

"She went out of town today for a couple days."

"Good." He strode up to Nic and kissed her, from the bottom of his soul, the way he'd been thinking of doing all day.

She melted against him instantly, her arms wrapping around his waist, her hands slipping inside his shirt, cold on his back.

He didn't care. He'd warm her up. "I need you. Now."

"The couch." She took his hand and pulled him into the living room.

He felt a stab of disappointment. She'd never invited him to her bed. He knew her room was sacred, but it bothered him that she lumped him in with the other men that she'd dated.

She'd also refused to show him her designs. He'd brought it up a couple times, but she'd bristled, so he avoided that topic. He didn't even bring up the fact that he'd give his left nut to see her in the black one.

He just had to convince her to trust him. After all, he was the one here with her — no one else.

She let go of him and pulled her top over her head, flashing him her impish smile.

Red lace—heaven help him. "Convenient that Susan's out of town," he said calmly as if he weren't bursting at the seams to be inside her. He unbuttoned his jeans.

She undid her pants, unzipped her boots, and pushed them all off in one swoop. "She travels a lot for work."

He took her in, the bare skin, the gentle curves. Admiring. In awe. "I am grateful."

"For?" Her hair cascaded down her back as she took her ponytail down.

"For Susan being gone. For you." He wrapped his arms around her waist, loving the feel of her, loving her scent. "For this. I don't want to take a moment with you for granted."

Her lips curved in that adorable crooked grin that hadn't changed. "We better get on it then," she said as she stripped bare.

Quickly taking his clothes off, he sat down and pulled her to straddle his lap.

She rubbed herself on him, her hands anchored on his shoulders. "You know what I'm grateful for?"

"Tell me."

"The chance to do this." She nibbled her way up his chest, his neck, spearing her fingers in his hair as she took his mouth.

He held her tight, needing to be closer, needing to be inside her. He lay back, pulling her over him.

She sat up and looked around. "Condoms?"

He cursed under his breath. He'd been in such a hurry to get her naked that he forgot to get them out. "In my bag."

Nicole stopped him from moving with a hand on his chest. "I'm on the pill, if you're safe."

Stilling, he stared at her. He wouldn't have trusted anyone else—Roddy had drummed caution into his head. But Nicole was different. He trusted Nicole with everything. "I'm safe," he said softly.

"Good." She reached between them and took hold of him.

The thought of sliding into her, no barriers,

had him breathless. He hissed as she slowly slid down on top of him.

"Okay?" she asked, easing herself down the rest of the way.

"Better than okay." He held her hip with one hand but gave her the room to move the way she wanted.

Sighing, she closed her eyes and dropped her head back. She rolled her hips back and forth against him. "I've been thinking of this all day."

Liking the husky timber of her voice, he reached his free palm to abrade the tips of her breasts. "Does it feel just like you imagined?"

"Better." She braced herself on his chest and rubbed herself up and down on him, over and over. The little sounds she made were so hot, and combined with the feel of her taking her pleasure with him had him ready.

He had to hold out—he wanted to watch her come first. He gritted his teeth and pushed his pelvis up.

She gasped, her fingers biting into his skin. Her eyes were still closed, but her head fell forward and the rocking of her hips became frantic.

"Yes, Nicole," he said softly, his hold on her firm. "Take me. I'm all yours, for your pleasure. Take it from me, Nicole."

She cried out, and he felt her tighten around him as she orgasmed.

It pushed him over the edge, too. His neck arched and he called out her name as his hips pushed up into her one last time.

She collapsed on his chest. He felt her heartbeat against his chest, and he cuddled her closer. They lay silently for a while, then he said, "I had a breakthrough today."

"Really?" She moved her head so she could look at him.

"I have one part of my song."

"That's great." Her smile didn't seem to reach her eyes. "And the lyrics too?"

"Some of them. Once I nail the music, the rest comes pretty quickly."

"I guess you'll be out of my hair soon," she said slowly.

"You don't sound happy about that." He tried not to feel hopeful but it was hard.

She shrugged, flipping her hair so it covered

her face. "This is a pretty ideal situation. I'll be sorry to see it end."

"Does it have to end?" he asked carefully.

Nicole shifted off him, sitting on the edge of the couch. "What are you saying?"

"Come with me." He sat up and took her hand. "My manager knows I'm in San Francisco, and it's only a matter of time until the real world crashes down on me. It'd be great to have you with me. I haven't felt this way in a long time."

"You're just in the afterglow of creativity."

Funny—KT had used that exact term. "It's more than that, Nic."

"What about my job?"

"It's in a lingerie store. You can come back to it or find another one to work in if you change your mind."

"It's not just a lingerie store. It's a community." She frowned. "I love working there."

But was it more important than he was? The insinuation irritated him. She never stuck with anything—he didn't see how that shop would be any different.

Not that he could point that out without risking becoming a eunuch, so instead he said, "What about designing your own lingerie?"

She recoiled as if he'd suggested killing puppies for a living.

"It can't be that far out from left field," he said. "You draw pictures of underwear all the time. You must have entertained the idea, even fleetingly."

"It's just something I like to do." She pulled her hand away. "It's not anything more than a way to pass time."

"Maybe it should be. The designs I saw were evocative. I could see them on you, and they'd look sexy as hell."

She stared at him like the Sphinx: mysterious and inscrutable. Finally she said, "Tell me about your song."

"You're changing the subject," he said, disappointed.

"It seems smartest."

"I don't know about that, but it's certainly safest."

She swallowed. "You like being safe."

"Yes, but sometimes you have to take a risk." He brushed her hair back, suddenly positive this was one of those instances.

But Nicole apparently didn't think so, because she gave him a flippant grin and slid back over him. "I say we get risky again, just you and me and this couch."

He let her engage him in a deep kiss, knowing she was trying to distract him as much as turn him on. So he kissed the breath out of her. If words didn't work, he'd show her they could be different. He was going to try his damndest to convince her, even if he wasn't sure she'd see it through and stick with it.

Chapter Seventeen

Rachel peeked her head into Romantic Notions after school, looking for Griffin Chase. No sign of him still.

Grrr. She made a face. At this rate she'd give him her mom's poem in time for the tenth anniversary of her death. The *sons* had given her a hard time about it again today. What else was new, right? Rachel wished she hadn't said anything to them, but the satisfaction when Griffin Chase used her poem would be so great.

If she could track him down.

"Hey there." The sales lady, Nicole, emerged from the back and smiled at her. "How are you?"

"Okay," she murmured, hunching her shoulders as she backed out of the store.

"How are your new bras?"

She stopped. "You remember me?"

"Of course I remember you. You bought the Elle Macpherson in two colors. How are they?"

She loved them actually. When she wore them, she felt like a grown up, and what the —*sons of anarchy* said bothered her less. "They're good."

Nodding, Nicole walked to a table on the side and started rummaging through a pile of lace. "I have another set I think you'd like. It comes in a berry color that'll look fabulous on you."

"I don't know that I need more underwear."

The woman held out the bra and panties. "Underwear isn't about need. It's about want. Try them on."

Her dad would probably be pissed when he saw the charges on his credit card—she probably shouldn't buy more.

Rachel stared at the pretty raspberry color. It looked like something her mom would have worn. Plus she felt powerful when she wore her pretty underthings, like it was her superhero suit.

Her dad was too wrapped up in his own life to notice anything about her, much less that she'd made a charge on his card.

"Okay," she said with a smile. Happy with the decision, she took underwear to the fitting room.

This time, she wasn't surprised when Nicole burst into her room. She turned her back and waited to be fixed.

"Perfect," the sales lady said as she adjusted the straps. "This style is really great on you. You have such a sweet figure."

She touched the tiny heart sewn on the strap, feeling so pretty. "I'll get it."

"Awesome." Nicole grinned at her. "I knew I recognized a fellow lingerie girl."

"What's that?"

"My boss always says that there are two types of women, those who love shoes and those who love lingerie. You're definitely a lingerie girl. I'll let you change."

Rachel waited till the curtain was closed before she changed back into her clothes. She felt so much better about life, even if she hadn't seen Griffin Chase. Picking up her bag, she parted the curtain and went out to the front.

Nicole was on the phone. "Grif and I are going

out tonight if you want to go with us," she was saying, her back turned.

Grif? As in Griffin Chase? Rachel froze and strained to hear.

"We're going to the Boom Boom Room, because a friend of his is playing there, probably around eleven o'clock." Nicole laughed and then nodded. "Okay, I'll talk to you later, Susan."

Griffin Chase was going to be at someplace called the Boom Boom Room tonight.

Rachel's breath caught with excitement in her chest. If she went there, she could give him the lyrics she'd written. And maybe he'd even sing. Maybe if she asked him, he'd sing to *her* specially. She'd bought a bunch of things from his best friend after all.

Nicole turned around. "Ready?"

"Yeah." She handed over the underwear. "Um, do you have another color, too?"

"I have a slightly different style in emerald." She strode to a dresser on the side and pulled out the drawer. "Green is this season's black."

Rachel looked at the bra the woman handed her. It looked like something a fairy would wear, lacy and delicate in a dark jewel color. She touched it. It was the sort of underwear a bold, unstoppable girl wore. Maybe she'd wear it tonight when she snuck into the Boom Boom Room. "I'll take it, too."

"I'll ring you up."

As Nicole rang her up, Rachel took out her phone and messaged Aaron. *What are you doing tonight?*

Two seconds later the reply came in: *Are you asking me out?*

She swallowed nervously and thumbed her screen. *Do you know a place called the Boom Boom Room?*

AARON HAWKE: *It's on Fillmore at Geary, but it's 21 and over.*

RACHEL ROSENBAUM: *Can we sneak in?*

AARON HAWKE: *Why?*

RACHEL ROSENBAUM: *There's a musician I want to see.*

AARON HAWKE: *Badly enough to sneak in.*

RACHEL ROSENBAUM: *Yes.*

She waited for what seemed like forever but he didn't reply. Finally, impatience won out.

RACHEL ROSENBAUM: *Well?*

AARON HAWKE: *I'll pick you up at 11. Don't wear neon.*

RACHEL ROSENBAUM: *I think you're safe on that count.*

AARON HAWKE: *You can never be too sure.*

"Here you go, Rachel." Nicole handed her the bag. "Welcome to the club."

The lingerie club wasn't the only one she was crashing. She took her package and went home. She had to figure out what to wear.

Her dad knocked on her bedroom door as she was getting ready. "Rachel?"

Her heart jumped into her throat. She froze, her jacket halfway on. "What is it?"

"I want to talk to you. Open the door."

She looked at herself in the mirror. She'd just

ringed her eyes in eyeliner, trying to look older, and she was fully dressed. It wouldn't have been an issue except her father didn't know she was going out. "Not now, Dad."

"Yes, now."

He was using that *I'll brook no argument from you* tone that meant he wouldn't budge until he spoke with her. Sighing, she kicked off her shoes as she shrugged out of the coat, smudging off some of the eyeliner. She threw her robe on her clothes and flung open the door. "Yes?"

He leaned in the doorway, arms crossed across a pastel polo shirt.

Pastel.

She pointed at his shirt. "What are you wearing?"

He frowned at her face. "What's that on your face?"

"Nothing." She rubbed under her eyes. "I was trying on makeup."

For some reason, he looked affronted. "You don't need makeup, Rachel. You're already pretty."

He picked *now* to act interested? "That's what you came here to say to me?"

He rolled his eyes. "No. I need to talk to you."

"I'll clean up my room tomorrow," she preempted, glancing at the time. Aaron was going to be here any minute, and she didn't want her dad to find out. Ever since the drunken party episode that landed them in San Francisco, she'd been on lockdown.

"That's not what I wanted to talk about. I wanted to talk about you and me."

Great. Just what she needed. *Not.*

"This is important." He stood straight and gestured to her room. "Can I come in?"

No way. "I'm kind of tired, Dad."

"Rachel, be a team player."

She hated when he talked corporate to her. She crossed her arms. "You have to be part of a team to be a team player."

He nodded. "I deserved that, but that doesn't mean you're getting out of this talk."

She really couldn't deal with this now. "Fine, but tomorrow."

"Tomorrow morning, before school." He pointed at her. "Don't think you can avoid me. I'm serious, Rachel."

"Okay." She rolled her eyes. "I heard you."

He rolled his eyes, too, muttering something about teenagers as he left.

Closing the door, she pressed her ear to it, listening to make sure her dad left. When she couldn't hear his footsteps, she quickly reapplied her makeup before Aaron arrived.

Did she look old enough? Rachel frowned at herself in the mirror and then decided to add a little more eyeliner. She wore all black, figuring it'd help her blend into the background, but really she mostly only had black anyway.

Griffin Chase wasn't going to notice her in black.

She'd make him notice her, she vowed silently. Not in a romantic way but because she wanted him to have what she'd written. She wasn't an idiot—she knew she was too young for Griffin Chase to like in any way other than just friendly. Unless he were into the Lolita thing, and based on his dating history she doubted that.

Plus, she had a feeling Nicole was into him. Rachel could totally see him digging on the lingerie lady. She was hot, with her skirts and boots.

Maybe one day Rachel would be hot like Nicole. She wondered what Aaron thought.

Her phone buzzed with a text. Aaron was here.

Nervous and excited, Rachel snuck downstairs, checking in her coat pocket to make sure her lyrics was still in there. She sighed when she felt the folded page.

At the top of the stairs, she heard voices from her dad's room. She paused, listening but not understanding what he was saying because he spoke so softly.

Who was he talking to? She frowned as her dad laughed, low and intimate.

Her phone buzzed again, and she hurried down the stairs and outside.

A black car waited at the curb. The car's door opened, and Aaron stuck his head out. "Your carriage, Cinderella."

Glancing back to make sure her dad hadn't seen her, she hurried to the car. "This is your dad's?"

"Uber," he said, scooting over to make room for her. "It's a driver service app."

"Spiffy." She nodded at the driver as she closed the door.

Aaron gave the driver instructions, and the car slowly pulled away. He turned to her. "Are you ready to live on the wild side?"

His face was so close to hers in the darkness that her breath caught. She looked into his eyes and swallowed thickly, only able to nod.

"Good." He grinned. "I've got a plan."

He had the driver drop them off around the corner and took her around the back of the club. There was a door open with a man guarding it. From inside, music poured onto the street, the energetic beat not helping her nerves.

"Wait." Aaron tugged her against the building, watching the doorway.

She shifted her weight from foot to foot, having doubts. Apparently she wasn't cut out for a life of crime.

"Now." Aaron pushed her toward the door. "Act natural."

Right. She rushed inside, noticing that the man who'd been guarding it was gone. Aaron tugged her down the short hall and right into the thong of people on the dance floor.

It was hot and stuffy, the air smelling like pot.

She blinked, not sure what to think about that. She'd only been around pot once, at that party that changed her entire life.

Focus, she told herself. Taking her coat off, she craned her head to look for Griffin Chase. It was dark, and the bar went all the way back and was packed with people. She stood on her tiptoes. She couldn't see anyone.

"This is great," Aaron said close to her ear. "I didn't know you liked Eric McFadden and his band."

She didn't even know who they were. She paused in her search to listen to the music. Actually, they *were* pretty good. She felt her feet start to tap to the music.

No, she needed to focus. She knew Griffin Chase was going to be here.

"Are you looking for someone?" Aaron asked, his breath tickling her ear.

She was going to deny it, but then she saw the interested way he looked at her, and she blurted, "Yes."

His brow furrowed. "Who?"

"Griffin Chase." She sighed. "I know you think

I'm crazy, but he's going to be here tonight and I have this poem to give him."

Rachel couldn't tell what Aaron was thinking, but then he nodded and said, "Then let's look around."

She blew out a breath she hadn't known she'd been holding. Smiling, she let him take her hand and walk her through the club.

Griffin wasn't there.

She bit her lip, disappointed.

Aaron squeezed her hand. "If he shows up, we'll see him. Let's dance and we'll keep an eye out for him."

Feeling hopeful, she smiled and nodded. They wedged their way onto the dance floor. He found an open pocket for them, faced her, and began to dance.

She'd never known a guy who'd willingly dance. She watched him, dumbfounded. She'd never danced with anyone but her mom. Her mom used to turn up the music and then they'd dance in the kitchen, crazy and uninhibited.

She hadn't danced since her mom died.

It felt good, she realized suddenly. She wondered if she should feel bad, but she could almost feel her mom smiling down at her, encouraging her to let herself be free.

So she did—she threw her arms in the air and let it loose, the way she used to with her mom.

Aaron whistled loudly and joined in, dancing every bit as enthusiastically as she was. She laughed when he did what he called the sprinkler, and she replied with a chicken dance.

"Let's not stop until the band stops," she yelled at him over the music.

He twirled her and then moved her into a dip. "I'll dance with you until you turn into a pumpkin, Cinderella."

The band only took a short break, playing until two in the morning. Sweaty but exhilarated, they reluctantly stopped, going outside for fresh air.

Aaron sat on the sidewalk. "I'll call an Uber."

She sat down next to him, feeling the waves of heat coming off him. She liked it and leaned closer even though she was really sweaty and gross.

"We didn't find Griffin Chase," Aaron said suddenly, looking at her.

Shrugging, she smiled. "It was still fun."

"Maybe we could do it again sometime," he asked carefully, his hand creeping closer to hers.

She froze. Was he going to hold her hand? She wiped it on her jeans, just in case.

But then the car arrived. Disappointed, not wanting the night to end, she reluctantly got in.

They didn't talk for the first few blocks, but then Aaron turned to her. "You've got moves. I didn't know, Rosenbaum."

His face was so close she was afraid to breathe. "You're the one with moves."

"Most people aren't lucky enough to witness them," he said modestly. He took her hand. "You're part of a privileged few."

The feel of his palm against hers robbed her of her thoughts. It was a lot of sensation, but at the same time she wanted more, even though she didn't know what that was.

He leaned toward her, and her body listed toward his. Was he going to kiss her?

Her breath caught in her throat, and she held it nervously. She'd never kissed anyone—not really, and definitely not like Aaron.

She really wanted to kiss him. She just wasn't sure what to do. Tongue? No tongue?

He leaned toward her, and their lips touched.

His were warm and dry and soft, still on hers. He made no move to maul her or to stick his tongue in her mouth the way Christian Murphy had at homecoming last year. It was like Aaron was waiting.

She should do something, like move her lips or something. She just wasn't sure what.

Then Aaron moved his lips, sliding them a little against hers.

The car door opened suddenly.

They both turned, and she froze when she saw her Dad's furious face looming in the door.

Chapter Eighteen

ARCHING, NICOLE LET the hot water soothe her back. She didn't know how Grif slept on that couch—two nights on it had her sore. Of course, it was tight with the two of them on it.

Frankly, even with the lack of space and the tight muscles, she didn't mind—not when it meant lying entwined with him all night. Not when he woke her up in the morning with bone-melting sex.

As Nicole turned the shower off and reached for her towel, she heard the softest strain of music.

Guitar music.

She froze and listened. It didn't sound like a recording, even though it was smooth and easy. It meant one thing: that Grif had picked up his guitar.

Wrapping the towel around her, she went to her doorway, closer but not so close that she'd interrupt him. She wanted to hear what he was playing.

She stilled, holding her breath. She hadn't heard this tune before. Was it the new one he was working on? She wouldn't admit it to anyone, but she was something of an expert on his music. His first album had been brilliant, and his next one had been good but not as innovative and fresh.

Not like whatever he was playing now.

It still sounded like him, with his signature simplicity and raw power, but this had a layer of dark longing that she hadn't heard from him before.

The music paused, and then he repeated one section. She wrapped the towel around her, securing the end, and went into the living room. "Play the whole thing for me again."

He started over without missing a beat, watching her the entire time. He played through to the refrain twice, then the next time he began to sing with the song. *"I'm here with you. Kiss me, take me, love me. I'm here for your pleasure, I'm here for you..."*

Goose bumps rose all over her arms. It felt like he sang it not just *to* her but *for* her. She shouldn't make a big deal out of it—it was what he did. He was expert at making people feel like he was singing just to them, even in a crowd of sixty-thousand people.

But *this* felt different. No matter how much her brain cautioned her heart, she just couldn't make it believe that this wasn't special. Like he sang it directly to her heart. At least her heart felt that way.

As though her heart belonged to him.

Her breath caught in her chest. *Panic.*

But it was silly to panic. She was overreacting. What she was feeling was the pull of great sex, not some elusive thing that she wasn't ready for.

He finished, trailing off, and she said, "Sing it again."

He tipped his head and began over.

She closed her eyes to listen to it this time, not wanting to be distracted by the intensity he aimed at her. She wanted to hear the song itself.

It was good. Really good. Even better than the first time.

She reopened her eyes as he began the refrain and sang along with him. *"I'm here with you now. Kiss me, take me, love me..."*

He stopped singing, letting her voice soar on its own. She sang what she remembered of the chorus, the last note trailing off with his guitar.

"You still have a great voice," he said.

She shrugged. "It's rusty. I only sing along to Pandora at work."

"Why is that? I've had backup singers who don't have the skill you do."

"Music's always been your thing, not mine. You have to have passion for it to make a living at it, like you do. I just don't have that in me."

"What do you have a driving passion for?"

Right now? Him.

Her parents always told her everyone had a purpose. It just took some people longer to figure out what theirs was. In the meantime you had to be open and try new things, because you never knew what might become a passion.

She'd never imagined Grif would become a passion.

But was it enough?

No. The answer was immediate and concrete. She knew she needed a passion that was all her own, and Grif would never be only hers. She needed something private, just for her.

She sat on the edge of the couch. "I think you don't realize how lucky you are to have known from childhood what you wanted to do with your life. It doesn't come so easy to everyone."

"You've been trying things for a long time," he pointed out. "Nothing's struck you?"

She liked to draw lingerie, but it seemed a long ways from having that be her calling. "I haven't found the right passion yet," she said finally.

"What about designing underwear?" he said, as if reading her mind.

"That's just something I do."

"And you're good at it. Really good at it. You wouldn't be able to draw like that if you didn't have a passion for it."

Just the thought of trying to launch a lingerie line made her hyperventilate. She didn't have the first clue how to go about it, much less manufacture the pieces. She shook her head. "It's just a hobby. I prefer working at Romantic Notions."

"Because it's safe." He set his guitar down. "How long are you going to stay there? You know you don't stick with any one thing for that long."

"It sounds like you're saying I'm a screw up." She crossed her arms. "Don't forget that you still had doubts even though you have a calling. You came here needing me to convince you to keep going with your music, so don't pretend you're so much better than me."

"I'm not saying that."

"That's not what it sounds like."

"I'm just saying how can you know if it's what you're supposed to do if you don't give anything a try? You move on before you can really commit to something."

"Like what?"

"Like—" He shook his head, visibly calming himself down. "I don't want to spend our time fighting, Nic."

Because they didn't have that many days left together. He didn't say it, but she got it nonetheless. He was pretty much done with his song. The music was all there, and he himself said the words would quickly follow. Their time was drawing to an end.

She'd known all along this day would come. She just thought she'd be prepared for it. She stood up, trying to hide her sadness. "I need to go to work."

He smiled a little as he strummed his guitar. "You might want to get dressed first."

Standing, she let out a sound that hopefully sounded like a chuckle. She shivered as she walked to her bedroom. She wasn't sure if it was from chilling in the damp towel or because of the disappointed way Grif stared at her.

Chapter Nineteen

RACHEL WOKE UP from a dream that Aaron had kissed her, and it'd been so great.

She sat up in bed, pushing the covers aside as she remembered the night before. Only it wasn't a dream. He *had* kissed her, and it'd been better than great. She started to smile—

But then she remembered the look on her dad's face when he caught them in the car.

The happiness she'd woken up with melted into dread. Last night, her dad hadn't said anything to her beyond a curt "Go to bed." Usually he was gone to work way before she got up, but she had a feeling this morning was going to be different.

She wondered if anyone would notice if she spent the next couple years hidden in her room.

Sighing, she forced herself to get out of bed. She washed the smeared eyeliner from under her eyes and made herself look as much like a good girl as she could. To give herself extra confidence, she wore one of her new bras and panties, topping them with a plain T-shirt and jeans.

As ready as she'd ever be, she decided, grabbing her bag and going downstairs.

Her dad was waiting for her in the kitchen. He didn't look up from his tablet even though she knew he knew she was standing there. He calmly took another sip of his coffee and swiped the screen.

Nerves twisted her gut. Normally he'd want to "parse" the situation and "come to a mutually beneficial resolution." The fact that he was so stony freaked her out. It meant he was pissed.

Swallowing, she shuffled to the table and slumped onto a chair. She couldn't believe it, but she'd give anything to hear him use those workplace words he liked that drove her crazy.

He swiped the screen again, his jaw tight.

She frowned, feeling the anger rise in her. He never paid attention to her. He didn't have the right to be pissed with her — it wasn't like he cared. "If you don't say anything, we're both going to be late."

He pushed the tablet aside and glared at her. "That's what you're going to open with?"

She crossed her arms. "What was I supposed to say?"

"Why don't you try *I'm sorry*?"

"That would imply that I regretted my actions." She felt a twinge of guilt at how bratty she sounded. Her mom never liked it when she took that tone.

Her dad set his coffee cup down so hard she was surprised it didn't crack. "I've had enough, Rachel. It's bad enough that you've been uncommunicative and difficult. Last night, you broke a trust. A tentative trust because you broke it before, by getting drunk at that party."

She winced — she couldn't help it. Getting drunk really had been stupid. "Last night was nothing like that party," she mumbled, sinking lower into her seat.

"You snuck out with a boy," her dad yelled, slamming his hand onto the table.

She jumped, her breath catching in her throat. Her dad never yelled. Ever. She gripped the edges of her chair's seat, not sure what'd happen next.

"Who knows what you were doing until three in the morning," he continued loudly. "All I know is you were making out in the back seat of that car."

"We weren't making out," she said sullenly. He made it sound so awful, and her first real kiss should have been one of the best memories of her teenage life. She may have snuck out, but she didn't do anything wrong. Not really anyway. Yes, she should have told him, but it wasn't like he'd been available lately.

"Give me a break, Rachel. I know kissing when I see it." He pushed back in his chair, making a shrill scratching sound on the floor. "Needless to say, you're grounded until further notice. Come home directly after school, no activities, no going out with friends."

But then she wouldn't be able to look for Griffin Chase. She sat up, feeling panicked for the first time. "But I have to —"

"This is non-negotiable, Rachel." Her dad

stared at her like she was a stranger he didn't like. "Iliana will be here in the afternoons to stay with you until I come home."

"I don't need a babysitter!"

"You should have thought of that before you acted the way you did last night."

"I didn't act in any way!" She got up and reached out. "I can explain what I was doing. It was for Mo —"

"I'm done, Rachel," her dad said over her. He scrubbed his face with his hand. "I understand how hard it was to lose your mom, because she was my world and I lost her, too. But I don't know what to do with you anymore. You're not helping me, and you're not giving me many options."

She gulped down a big wad of shame. And fear, because she'd never heard him sound so defeated before. "What are you talking about?"

He looked at his watch. "I'm late for a meeting."

She started after him. "But Dad —"

The look he gave her stopped her in her tracks. "Rachel, I'm done," he repeated. "I'm having dinner with a friend. I'll be home late."

"What friend?" She hated that he had a life and she didn't, that he seemed happy and she was miserable. She narrowed her eyes, remembering him laughing intimately in his bedroom late last night. "Are you going out on a date?"

"Yes, it's a date."

"How could you?" she yelled. "You're being unfaithful to Mom!"

"Your mom is dead, Rachel!" he yelled back.

Silence.

They stared at each other, shocked. Rachel touched her cheek, feeling like he'd slapped her.

Her dad opened his mouth like he was going to say something more, but then he shook his head and strode out.

She watched him until she couldn't see him any more.

He didn't mean all that stuff. Well—yes, he did, but he didn't have all the facts. She'd tell him enough to make him feel better, and then he'd let her out of lockdown so she could get back to finding Griffin Chase.

As she reached for her bag, her sleeve touched her dad's tablet and the screen woke up. She took her bag and was about to go to school when two words jumped out at her: boarding school.

She gaped at the screen. Turning it around she quickly scanned the web page. *A boarding school for troubled teenagers*.

She dropped back onto the chair. He was going to send her away.

She was halfway to school when she realized there was no reason to go.

Rachel stopped in her tracks. He was going to send her to boarding school—and it made her heart *hurt*—what did it matter if she screwed up in school?

It didn't.

She turned around and headed for Romantic Notions. She'd wait for Griffin Chase instead. If she had to leave, at least she could make sure she did this one last thing for her mom.

The wind was super cold. She sat on the curb and watched the store for as long as she could before she had to admit defeat and go inside Grounds for Thought. Fortunately, there was a small table open in the front window. She put her stuff there and went to order a hot chocolate.

The blonde who was always there manned the counter. Tucking her hair behind her ear, she smiled at Rachel. "No school today?"

"Not really," she mumbled, pretending to study the pastries even though she already knew what she wanted.

"Hot chocolate?" the lady asked. "And I recommend the chocolate chip Madeleines today. I know if you order Madeleines, you're probably a purist, but trust me, the chocolate chip ones are to die for."

She shrugged. "Okay."

The blonde took her money. "My name is Eve, by the way. What's your name?"

"Rachel," she murmured, putting her change away.

"I'll bring your cookies and drink out to you, Rachel."

"Thanks." She went to take her seat to begin her vigil. She watched the dark store for five minutes before it occurred to her that Nicole wouldn't be arriving until later, so she took out her blank notebook, a pen, and her phone.

There were a bunch of text messages from Aaron, asking if she was okay.

She was going to be sent to boarding school, and she'd never get to kiss Aaron again. Even if she came back, why would he want to hang out with someone who'd been imprisoned?

Putting her phone away, she stared at the notebook. If only her mom were here, none of this would have happened.

Although if her mom were here, she wouldn't have met Aaron either. Or Griffin Chase.

She frowned.

"Here you go, Rachel." Eve set the hot chocolate on the table with a little plate of cookies. "Anything else you need?"

She looked up at the café lady, who had no idea what she was asking. Feeling sad, she shook her head and pulled the hot chocolate closer.

Eve hesitated for a moment, but someone walked in, so she went to take their order. Just as well. Rachel didn't feel like talking.

But she could write.

She pulled out her laptop and opened her email.

To: jim.rosenbaum@valleytechnology.com
From: rachel_rose@gmail.com
Subject: I KNOW.

You're going to send me away to boarding school???

How could you?? When were you going to tell me? As you and your girlfriend got married?

How can you just forget Mom and move on? Don't you love her anymore? Don't you think about her at all??

I think about her ALL THE TIME. I feel like if I don't, I'll forget her, and if I forget her then no one will know how great she was. Remember that time she surprised you with a picnic at work, and how we sat on the floor of your office, and she brought sparkling grape juice so it was like a celebration? It was for no reason except that she loved you. She always did stuff like that, just because, to make a person feel good.

And you're trashing her memory!

Well, I won't forget her, and if that's a crime you might as well send me away.

Maybe it's just as well, because now you can start fresh with a new family. You don't need reminders of the past hanging out. Your girlfriend probably won't like me. I'm not sure you do anymore either.

Rachel reread the email, her cursor hovering over *Send*. But then she clicked delete, closed her laptop, and put her head down on the table. He didn't care—why even bother?

Chapter Twenty

*A*s SHE WALKED up onto Grounds for Thought, Nicole found Marley and Valentine already sitting at their usual table. She waved at them through the window and went in to join them. She was really late.

Grif's fault. He'd told her he wanted to make sure he hadn't neglected any part of her, and he'd been very diligent about keeping his word. She'd replied that maybe he needed to double-check a couple areas. He'd risen to the challenge.

The passion was only minorly dimmed by the argument they'd had about her career. They had an unspoken truce, but everything hung heavy between them—especially the fact that Grif would be leaving soon.

But she wasn't going to think about that. She

was going to enjoy Marley and Valentine, who stood as Nicole approached.

"You're back," Nicole exclaimed, catching her up in a big hug.

"Yesterday." Her friend smiled wide. She had a glow from sun and love that lit her skin. "Ethan says hi."

Marley shook her head. "You know I can't call him that, right? And I'm also not sure I can stand to hear sex stories about him."

Nicole took off her jacket and hung it on the back of her seat. "I want to hear sex stories. After I get a mocha."

"A mocha." Marley raised her brow. "Feeling decadent?"

More like she needed a pick-me-up. She was a happy person, but the past few days she'd been up and down. Mostly because of Grif harping on her designs, but also because he was going to leave.

She didn't want him to.

But she flashed a Cheshire smile to put up a brave front and went to order her drink. When she came back, she took a seat and waved her hand. "I'm ready for sex."

"You're not my type." Valentine grinned. "I missed you guys. What have you been up to?"

Nicole swiped whipped cream with her finger and licked it. "First we need to hear about the honeymoon."

"But the PG version," Marley said.

"Then it'll be a short discussion." Valentine smiled, her cute dimples flashing. "I thought we were just going to drive down the coast, but he surprised me by taking me to Tahiti."

"Tahiti." Nicole sighed. "That's so romantic."

"We stayed at this resort that was beautiful, in a private villa with our own swimming pool, and it was warm, and we didn't need swimsuits."

Marley stuck her fingers in her ears. "La la la la la…"

Laughing, Nicole pushed her friend's hands back down. "As if you and Brian live chastely."

"Not at all. Brian's a sex machine," she said proudly. "But Valentine is like Pollyanna, and who wants to hear about Pollyanna having sex?"

"Are you saying I'm not sexy?" Valentine frowned, clearly affronted. "Ethan thinks I am."

"He thinks the sun rises and sets on you, too.

But you know who I do want to hear about?" Marley faced Nicole. "Griffin Chase."

"The rock star?" Valentine's little nose wrinkled. "Why would you care? You never even read the tabloids."

"I care because Nicole cares." Marley watched her, waiting expectantly.

Nicole lifted her cup, trying to act nonchalant.

Valentine shook her head. "Why would Nicole care? Does this have to do with his engagement?"

"Engagement?" Marley lurched forward, mouth gaping. Then she pointed at Nicole. "You've been holding out."

"No." She shook her head. "There's no engagement."

"Yes, there is. I read it in a celebrity magazine on the plane ride back yesterday." Valentine pursed her lips. "*People*, I think. Griffin Chase is marrying Inga."

"The Swedish supermodel?" Marley frowned.

Nicole shook her head again. "No, he's not."

"Did he tell you he wasn't?" Marley asked.

"No. But he also didn't tell me he was." He'd have told her, right? Because she was his best friend. Because they were having sex. He wouldn't have sex with her if he were engaged to someone else, even if he *was* leaving.

Valentine looked back and forth between them. "I don't understand what's going on here."

"Did you seriously not notice at your wedding reception?" Marley gaped incredulously. "I thought everyone noticed when Griffin Chase walked in."

"I was a little busy that night." Valentine frowned. "It doesn't make sense. Why would Griffin Chase be at my wedding?"

"Because Nicole is getting it on with him," Marley said tactfully.

"*What?*" Valentine whirled to face her.

Nicole shrugged. "That's technically not true. I started getting it on with him way after your wedding."

"When did this happen? *How* did this happen? And why does it always happen when I'm out of town?"

"This is the first time you've been out of town," Marley pointed out.

"Whatever." Valentine waved her hand. Then she faced Nicole. "I don't understand why the news is all over his engagement to Inga if you're dating him."

Dating seemed like overstating things. Except that they *had* been spending every minute she wasn't at work together. "It's just a mistake."

Valentine shook her head, leaning over and pulling out her phone from her purse. Thumbs flying, she held out the screen. "See?"

The headline on the web page read *Chase Catches Supermodel.*

"It's just one sensational article," Nicole said calmly.

Valentine shook her head, punched a couple more things on her phone, and then held it out again. The screen had a list of article headlines:

CHASE AND INGA ENGAGED!

ROCK STAR AND SUPERMODEL TO TIE THE KNOT

INGA AND GRIFFIN TO ENTER THE LEXICON OF ROCKER/
MODEL UNIONS

INGA SAYS IT'S A SUMMER WEDDING

Nicole read them all carefully—twice—and shook her head. "It's not true."

"Uh-oh," Marley said.

"What?"

She exchanged a look with Valentine, who said, "You've passed the point of no return."

"You're delusional," Marley added.

"I am?" Nicole looked down at herself. "I don't feel delusional."

Marley looked at her over the rim of her mug. "Trust us. In the dictionary, next to *delusional*, there's a picture of you."

"All these sources wouldn't report something that wasn't true," Valentine added gently.

Nicole shook her head. "I appreciate your concern. I really do. But there are always false reports about celebrities. Do you really think Kim Kardashian was impregnated by aliens?"

"This article wasn't in *The Enquirer*," Valentine said. "It's in *People*."

Nicole shrugged. "To-may-toes, to-mah-toes. And haven't you seen how this happens in the movies all the time? The heroine always believes the false report, and it breaks them up, but in the end the hero was innocent."

"So you believe Griffin Chase is innocent?" Marley asked, her brow raised skeptically.

"Grif wouldn't be with me if he were engaged to someone else."

"Hmm," Marley hummed noncommittally.

Nicole patted her friend's hand. "I sound like a smitten woman, I know, but it's not like that."

Marley and Valentine exchanged another look.

Nicole grinned. "It really isn't. He's not a douchebag."

"He's a musician," Marley pointed out. "Douchebag is practically synonymous."

"I don't believe it. He's always been solid. He'd have told me if he were engaged."

"Fine." Marley rolled her eyes. "When you're devastated because he's marrying a supermodel, just remember that I suck at the touchy-feely stuff. But because you're my friend, if you need to—I don't know—cry or something, I'll try not to panic."

Nicole laughed. "You're a pal."

Marley nodded. "I really do try."

꠸   ꠸   ꠸

They lay in her bed together. He sprawled out length-wise, and her head dangled off the side. Their clothes were strewn all over the floor, including the new purple Mimi Holliday set she'd wanted to show off to Grif. In his defense, he *had* admired it for a few seconds before stripping it off her.

She almost hadn't worn the new lingerie. She'd had a niggle of unease since the conversation with Marley and Valentine, and she didn't want to distract from it. But in the end, she knew she was just being paranoid. In fact…

She turned and slid up against his body, nestling her head on his shoulder. "I saw a funny story today."

He played with a strand of her hair. "What sort of funny story?"

"About you, being engaged to that supermodel Inga."

His body stiffened, not very much but enough that she noticed. "Where did you see the news?"

"All over." She chuckled. "It was detailed, with statements from your manager as well as Inga."

"It's not true."

She hadn't realized she'd been holding tension in her shoulders all day until right then. She rubbed his chest, feeling a surge of possessiveness that went hand-in-hand with joy. "I know. I didn't believe it."

"But we were engaged."

"What?" She sat up, frowning.

He propped himself on his elbow. "I broke it off before coming here. It was momentary insanity. It was never going to work with Inga, with the way we were both constantly jetting off in opposite directions."

"You were *engaged*?" she repeated, sounding shrill to her own ears. "For how long?"

"It doesn't matter—"

"Of course it matters." Pulling away, she sat up on her knees. "You loved her enough to *propose* to her. How does that not matter? That's huge. You don't just propose to someone. You obviously thought you could spend the rest of your life with her."

"I broke up with her, Nicole," he said, sitting up. "I obviously didn't believe it'd work."

"You broke up with her and then came here to see me." She crossed her arms, glaring. "So what does that make me? The other woman? The rebound? None of these answers are good."

He reached for her. "Nic—"

"No." She scrambled away from him. "Marriage is forever. You yourself said you wanted what your parents have. You must have thought you'd get it with Inga."

"I was wrong." He held his hand out, his gaze steady on her. "Just hear me out, okay?"

She glared at him, waiting.

Exhaling, he brushed his hair back. "I thought Inga was everything I could want, but there were things that were seriously missing. Intimacy, for one. And she didn't understand why I'd want to tour instead of follow her around and serenade her. In the end, she was a blip on the radar. This is just a publicity ploy by my manager and Inga."

She nodded stiffly. "Is my name going to end up in the magazines, too?"

He shook his head. "No."

"Does that make what happened between us

more real, or less true? Because it seems like maybe *this* is a blip on the radar."

"No." He stood up. "You're not like that, Nic."

"What am I then? You said you were going to leave, so how am I any different?" Except that she didn't rate a proposal.

That hurt—way more than she'd thought it would.

Grif stepped toward her. "I want you to come with me."

"You didn't want to tag along and follow Inga all over the world, but you're asking me to do the same thing? How does that make sense? And what would I do? Be the dependent girlfriend? Or worse, the chick who's having sex with the star without any promise of anything?"

"You're free, Nicole. There's nothing holding you here."

"What about my job?"

"What about your designs?"

"Not this again."

"Yes, this again." He frowned. "Maybe it's time you did something you actually cared about."

"I care about Romantic Notions."

"But it's not yours." He grabbed his jeans off the floor and pulled them up. "You have a real talent for designing. I may not know anything about fashion, but I can tell when something's good, and yours are amazing. It's up your alley, too. You love romance. But you aren't going to go for it. You're going to let the real thing pass you by, because you're scared to do it."

"I am not," she said tightly, even as part of her knew he was right.

He tugged his T-shirt over his head. "You're scared to go for that, and you're scared to go for us. Because whatever you think this is about, it's only about the fact that you aren't willing to give us a chance."

She yanked her robe off the hook on her door. "I knew nothing good would could come from this fling."

He paused, staring at her. The hurt in his eyes stung her heart. "See, Nicole, that's where we're different. This was never a fling to me. This was as real as it gets. To me, this was love."

She froze, barely able to breathe.

He lifted the necklace from his neck and set

it on her bedside table. Without a word he strode from her room.

She watched him leave, and then she stared at the arrowhead she'd given him so long ago and knew she'd lost her best friend forever.

Chapter Twenty-one

THE FIRST THING Nicole thought when she opened her eyes in the morning was that something was wrong.

It could have been because of her queasy stomach or throbbing head. She slowly eased her feet onto the floor, holding her forehead to keep her brains from sloshing around.

Then it all came back to her. The fantastic sex. The rumors of Grif's engagement. The argument. Grif leaving, and the subsequent night of debauchery Susan had insisted on, involving way too much wine.

Nicole looked at the bedside table. The arrowhead she'd given him lay there. Any vague hope she'd had that last night was all a dream vanished in a poof.

But maybe he'd come back. She slipped it over her head and stumbled out of her room to the living room.

It was pristine. No one sleeping on the couch, no pile of random hats and sunglasses, no guitar tucked in the corner.

He was gone.

She deflated.

Susan walked out of the kitchen, her hand outstretched with a steaming cup. "You look like how I feel. Why did I think all that wine was a good idea?"

"He's really gone," Nicole said out loud, taking the cup her roommate pushed into her hands. She absently sipped the coffee, not caring when her tongue burned.

"You wanted him gone, remember?" Susan curled into a corner of the couch, her feet tucked under her. "Last night, you were all 'To hell with him and his supermodel slut!'"

She winced. "Are you sure I said that?"

"Yep." Susan smiled faintly, cuddling her own mug to her chest. "You were on a roll. If he were here, I think you'd have punched him in the face."

"He proposed to her." She sank onto the couch and dropped her head back as all the emotions came back to her.

"I don't know if I should be saying this now, but maybe you're overreacting about the whole engagement thing."

"No, I'm not." She managed enough energy to glare at her roommate. "You don't propose to someone randomly, not unless you think you want to be with them forever."

"Not everyone has the same view of marriage as you do."

"Grif does. We talked about it." She dropped her head in her hands. "He asked me to go with him."

"*What?*" Susan gaped. "You never mentioned that."

"Because of course I wasn't going to go. But that's not the point."

"What's the point?"

"He didn't want to marry *me*. He just asked me to tag along with him, since I wasn't doing anything important here anyway."

"He said that?" Susan asked, sounding skeptical.

"Pretty much."

"Are you sure?"

She frowned at her roommate. "Whose side are you on?"

"Yours, which is why I'm going to say this." Susan pointed at her. "You like him, the kind of like that leads to the happy ever after you've always dreamed of. And whatever he said or has done, he likes you the same way. If you let him go, you'll regret it."

"But he doesn't —"

"Then make him." Throwing her arms in the air, Susan stood up. "Go after him. Tell him he's being an idiot. Sometimes the hero needs to be saved, Nicole."

She blinked at her roommate. "Beauty saved the beast."

"Exactly. So do it."

Nicole watched Susan stride out of the room, still mumbling to herself. She stayed on the couch, thinking about what her roommate had said.

Did Grif need to be saved?

She shook her head. She couldn't think about this now — she needed to get ready for work.

Going through the motions, she showered and dressed, feeling less like she was run over by a truck. A couple ibuprofen and her red boots and she was ready to face the world.

Mostly.

She considered stopping at Grounds for Thought for a doubly-fortifying dose of caffeine and a chocolate croissant, but she didn't want to run into anyone and have to explain why her eyes were so bloodshot, so she went directly to work.

Thankfully, it was a typically slow morning. Grateful for Olivia's foresight in installing a chime to announce customers, Nicole went to lie down on the floor in the largest dressing room, knowing she'd hear if someone came in.

She was on the floor with her arm over her eyes when her phone rang. It was her mom, based on the ringtone. She jumped to answer it. "Mom?"

There was a pause. "What's wrong, sweetheart?"

Tears came to her eyes. "Did you talk to Mrs. Chase?"

"No, I was just calling to say hi, but I can hear it in your voice."

"Grif left." She pinched the bridge of her nose to keep the tears in.

"What happened? Did he finish his song?"

"We had an argument."

"Was it about the reports of his engagement in the papers?"

"You saw those?"

Her mother chuckled. "The entire world saw them. Lottie was upset about it. She must be the only mother in the world who wasn't looking forward to a supermodel daughter-in-law. She came over on a rampage."

Nicole cracked a smile at that. She could see it. "Remember the time Grif's seventh grade English teacher gave him a C on a creative essay for not following directions, and she went to school and ripped the teacher a new one?"

Her mom laughed. "She's protective of her boy. But even she's upset with him over this. I told her I didn't think the rumors were true. Grif wouldn't lead you on that way."

"The rumors aren't true right now, but they were a year ago." She pouted, feeling her heart wither. "Mom, do you think marriage is forever?"

"It depends on the people, sweetheart."

"For me?"

"Are you getting married and I didn't know it?"

"Not apparently."

"Nicole—" Her mom paused. "Nicole, I always thought you and Griffin would find your way to each other eventually. We were all surprised that you didn't date in high school. You two connect in a way that's rare. I don't really know what you two argued about, but just think about if it was worth a life without him."

"I've spent the past nine years without him."

"Yes, but he came back to you."

The door signaled someone coming in. Nicole sat up and heaved herself off the floor. "I've got a customer, Mom."

"Think about it, sweetheart. I love you."

"Love you, too," she said as she ended the call and stepped into the store. She'd expected to see a customer, but Bull stood at a table, holding up a crimson merrywidow.

"I need to find a woman to buy this for." Grinning, he held it up to himself, but then his grin faded into a frown and he lowered his hands. "What's wrong?"

She shook her head. "I didn't think I looked that bad."

"You do." He tossed the merrywidow on the table. "It doesn't help that it looks like a funeral home in here, with all the flowers."

"It's out of control, isn't it?" But part of her loved all the flowers Grif had sent her, especially now that Julie had stopped bringing them around.

Bull charged toward her. Anyone else might have been intimidated by his bulk coming at her like that, but Nicole knew he was a big softie. He stood before her, his hands on his hips, looking fierce. "I love Griffin Chase's music, but give me the word and I'll break all his fingers."

"You're sweet." She patted his chest reassuringly and got on her tiptoes to kiss his cheek. "It's okay though. It was a losing proposition anyway."

"Why?"

She blinked. "What do you mean?"

"Why was it a losing proposition?" He scowled. "Didn't you like him?"

"Stop looking at me like that." She frowned at

him. "If that's the look you give your opponents, it's a wonder they don't pee their pants before you fight."

His eyes narrowed. "You're avoiding my question."

She threw her arms in the air. "Yes, I like him. Satisfied?"

"I'm not the one who looks like she went on a bender because someone stole her teddy bear," he retorted.

"My teddy bear walked away of his own accord," she threw back at him.

"What'd you do?"

She blinked. "Why did I have to do something?"

"Because the man looked at you like you were his world. If he left, it's because you pushed him away."

"He didn't try to push back."

Bull rolled his eyes. "Men are knuckleheads. Don't you women learn that early in life?"

Susan's words echoed in her head: *Sometimes the hero needs to be saved.*

Did Grif need to be saved?

It was why he came to her, wasn't it?

She stood up like she was jolted. *It was why he came to her.*

"I've gotta go. I'm supposed to meet E and Valentine. Your friend had some ideas about how I can market and sell my smoothies." He patted her on the head. "Don't be an idiot."

"Words to live by," she said dryly.

"Dude." He winked at her. As he turned to leave, he stopped and stared at the merrywidow he'd admired. He pointed at it. "Wrap one of these up for me. I want the largest size you've got. The panties, too."

"I thought you didn't have a girlfriend."

"I don't," he said as he took his wallet out. "But now I have a goal. To find a woman to wear that for me."

Shaking her head, she found him the largest size and rang him up nonetheless. He'd do it, too—she had no doubt. She didn't know him well, but she could tell he was the sort of person who went after what he wanted.

She always thought she was the same type of person.

The problem was she didn't know what she wanted.

She shook her head. That wasn't true—she wanted Grif. But she wanted him in a way that'd work. Following him around like a lovesick groupie wasn't going to cut it even in the short term.

Her gaze fell to the sketchpad she kept behind the counter. Grif hadn't understood why she didn't become a designer.

She took it out and flipped through it, trying to see the designs objectively. Only it was hard to see anything beyond the fear that gripped her throat.

She swallowed it down and put the sketchpad away. There was no way she could be a lingerie designer. She had no training, she just knew what she liked—it was crazy even to think about it.

Just as crazy as believing she could keep a world-renowned rock star happy when she wasn't even sure what made *her* happy.

Chapter Twenty-two

NICOLE PACED IN Romantic Notions, in the narrow lanes between the dressers and tables.

Three days.

Three days since Grif left.

Three days of sadness.

Three days of excessive thinking, which was totally *not* her style.

Three days, and still no answers.

She heaved a huge sigh. If she went on like this, she was going to go crazy, not to mention that Grif would eventually find another woman who'd want him enough to give everything up.

He didn't need a woman like that. He needed a woman who had a backbone, who had life in her. Who existed beyond Grif and his world.

Nicole wanted to be that woman.

She shook her head. How could she have ever doubted that? He came to her for help. He pretty much admitted she had what he needed, and she sent him away.

She sent away the one man she'd loved all her life.

She smacked her forehead.

The door jingled as someone entered. She whirled around, heaving a sigh of relief. "Valentine, I'm *so* happy to see you. I need help."

"That's what I gathered from your text." The former matchmaker unwrapped her scarf and flashed her impish grin. "All the exclamation points after the word *help* were a clue."

"I didn't want to be vague." She hugged her friend and then held her at arm's length. "I need a passion."

"You've got more passion in you than most people I know."

"But I don't stick with anything." Nicole let go and began to pace again. "I'm screwed up, which doesn't make sense at all because my parents have always been wonderful and supportive."

"Some chicks stay in the nest longer."

She stopped and stared at her friend.

Valentine shrugged. "I'm no good at analogies, but that's not the point."

"No, the point is I'm twenty-eight years old and still don't know what I want to be when I grow up."

"What brought this on?" Valentine set her purse on a table. "You've always been happy. Since the day we met, I've envied you because it's like life doesn't touch you. What happened?" Then her eyes widened. "Griffin Chase."

"He did something to me. The thing is, I think I needed it." Exhaling to get rid of her nerves, she waved at the counter. "Look at it and tell me what you think."

"At what? This sketchbook?"

She nodded grimly, averting her eyes because she didn't think she could deal seeing her friend's expression as she went through the designs. Valentine had started off as a matchmaker because of a family obligation, but it turned out she really had a brilliant business mind. She'd helped her husband launch a line of protective gear for fighters, and she herself designed apps for the iPhone.

Turning her back, Nicole fiddled with one of the displays, trying not to listen to the crinkle of pages as Valentine turned them. But it went on and on, and she knew there weren't *that* many designs, so finally she whirled around. "You're killing me!"

Valentine looked up, her large eyes blinking in surprise. She pointed at the pad. "These are great."

Nicole wilted. "You aren't just saying that?"

"Of course not."

"Do you think"—swallowing her fear, she asked the question quickly—"Icouldstartmyown-lingerieline?"

"What?" Valentine asked, her brow furrowing.

"Start my own lingerie line." She put a hand to her heart, afraid it was going to beat out of her chest. "Is it worth it to try?"

Valentine's expression softened. "It's always worth it to try, Nicole."

"Not if you're going to fail."

"How do you know if you'll fail if you don't try?" Valentine shook her head. "Or just decide you're going to make it happen. Why do you have to fail?"

She frowned. "Good point."

"I don't know what it takes to get a lingerie line started, but let me do a little research." Valentine took out her ever-present phone and began tapping at it. "In the meantime, I need you to put together a business plan."

"A business plan." She nodded, even though she had no idea how to do it or what it encompassed. "Okay."

Valentine grinned. "Look up samples online. Basically, you just want to declare that you're going to conquer the world, and how you plan to do it one panty at a time."

"I can do that." She nodded. Then she threw her arms around her friend. "I love you."

"You'll love me more when I turn you into a lace mogul." Valentine's expression became somber. "I think this lingerie idea is perfect for you, but I'm not sure how it's going to get you Griffin Chase."

She cleared her throat. "I was going to mention that I need to run my business from wherever I am in the world."

Valentine smiled slowly. "So you're free to travel with him all over. I like it. Make that one of the stipulations."

The front door chimed, and they both looked up to find Eve in the doorway.

Nicole knew Eve mostly from Olivia, because they were such good friends, but she'd always liked the café owner, even though Eve was a shoe girl rather than a fellow lingerie aficionado.

"You've got a stalker," Eve said. She smiled. "I think it's innocuous, but I thought I should let you know."

Grif? Nicole frowned. It couldn't be. She knew from her mom, who'd heard from Grif's mom, that Grif was in L.A. recording the rest of his album. "Who is it?"

"A teenager named Rachel."

"Rachel?" She blinked in surprise. "Small girl, dark hair, sad eyes?"

"You know her?"

"Yes, but she doesn't seem like a stalker." Nicole looked at Valentine.

Who hugged her. "Go. I'll get started on my research. Let's meet tomorrow after you get off work."

A lightning bolt of fear shot through her, but it was laced with excitement. She nodded even though she kind of felt like throwing up. "Tomorrow after work."

"Good girl." Valentine beamed at her. "I have a good feeling about this, Nicole. Prepare to become a mogul."

"I'd settle for making a living doing something I love." She walked them out of the store and locked it up. "Thanks, Valentine."

But her friend was already walking back to her apartment, in a daze, fiddling with her phone.

She shrugged and turned to Eve. "Rachel's in Grounds for Thought?"

"She was when I left." The blonde sighed. "I think she's cutting school. She's been in there every day this week, from early until about three. And she looks like she lost her best friend."

Nicole's heart bled for the girl. She understood what that was like.

They walked into the café. Eve nodded to the front window, where Rachel sat alone, staring at a notebook open in front of her. Giving Nicole's arm a squeeze, she retreated to the counter.

Taking a deep breath, Nicole strode to the teenager's table, pulled out the chair across from her, and sat down.

Looking up, Rachel's mouth dropped open.

Nicole hid her amusement. "I hear you might be planning to rob Romantic Notions."

"Aaron said the same thing," the girl mumbled, slumping in her seat. "But I'm not."

Something was very wrong. Rachel had seemed sad each occasion they'd interacted, but something was different now. She seemed beaten—not physically, but emotionally.

Not sure how to proceed, Nicole decided to start off light. "You mean you don't like your new underwear enough to rob the store?"

The girl blinked, then she pushed her shirt's collar aside to bare a polka-dotted strap. Leaning forward, she said, "I really am a lingerie girl. I think my mom was, too, because she had drawers full of underwear."

"Lingerie girls are the best." Nicole smiled.

"My mom was the best."

The way she said it, Nicole knew the girl had lost her mother. She imagined not having her mom around, and she had to swallow the sudden sadness. "How long has it been?" she asked somberly.

"A year and a half." Rachel looked up at her with eyes stark with pain. "They say it gets better, but I think they lie."

She nodded. "If my mom died, I'd be devastated."

"I know, right?" The teenager leaned forward. "No one gets it. They keep telling me I'll get over it, but that's stupid."

"At the same time, you have to learn to live with it," Nicole said delicately. "Your mom wouldn't want you to have a crappy life because you missed her. Think about it."

Rachel frowned, toying with the corner of a page in a blank notebook. "She wouldn't like me torturing my dad either, but he's not being nice to me either. He's *dating* someone."

Nicole tried to picture her dad dating someone else, and her stomach clenched painfully. "But you don't want him to be miserable and loveless for the rest of his life, do you? Does he deserve that?"

"No," came the grudging answer. The girl

looked up with blazing eyes. "She won't be my mom though."

"If she's smart, I bet she'll just want to be your friend, and it's always nice to have more friends."

Rachel didn't look convinced but she nodded.

"So." Nicole tipped her head. "Why have you been sitting here, watching the store?"

The girl hesitated, but then she visibly gave up. "I was waiting for Griffin Chase."

Weren't they all? Nicole shook her head ruefully. "He left."

Rachel looked so crestfallen that she wished she could take her words back, even though they were true.

"Is he coming back?"

Nicole shrugged. "Did you want his autograph?"

"I wanted to give him this." She pulled out a mangled piece of paper from her pocket. Spreading it open, she pushed it across the table.

Nicole picked it up. A poem. She read it quickly, surprised that it was actually good if heartbreaking. "Did you write this?"

"For my mom." She girl swallowed audibly.

"She loved Griffin Chase, and I thought if I could get him to sing a song for her..."

Nicole heart broke. "Can I take this?"

Rachel shrugged. "He's gone. It's not like it matters."

"I'll make sure he gets it."

The teenager gaped at her.

"I mean it," Nicole said. "I can't promise he'll put it in a song, but he'll get it. At the very least, I'll make sure he signs it and sends it back to you."

The girl continued to just stare at her. Then she jumped up and grabbed Nicole in a hug.

She hugged Rachel back, sad for her, but optimistic. "You're lovely, Rachel. I didn't know your mom, but I bet she'd be sad if you just gave up on life because she was gone. She wouldn't want that."

Rachel buried her head in Nicole's shoulder, holding her tight, her body shaking. Then she stood upright, wiping her face and nodding. "You're right. She'd be totally angry at me for how things are."

"Then fix them." Nicole smiled. "At the core, we lingerie girls believe in dreams coming true."

"Okay," Rachel said tentatively. Then she straightened her spine and said more firmly, "Yes. I'll fix it all."

"Good."

She looked at Nicole hopefully. "Did you really mean it about Griffin Chase?"

"Yes." She sighed. "But I'm not on his list of preferred people, so I can't guarantee much."

"You're a lingerie girl," Rachel said. "You just said we make our dreams happen."

"You're right." Nicole smiled, sitting up straighter, too. "I should listen to myself more often."

Chapter Twenty-three

RACHEL ENDED UP spending the day at Romantic Notions. Nicole told her she could help with displays as long as she promised that she wouldn't cut any more school.

It was an easy promise to make.

Nicole's boss, Olivia, came in early in the afternoon with her baby Parker. Rachel had no idea what to do with him at first—she'd never been around small kids—but he was so cute with his big bright eyes and gurgly laugh that she decided he was okay, even if he did drool on her.

Olivia had been super nice, too. She and Nicole even discussed letting Rachel work there for a couple hours two or three days a week. Rachel had wanted to throw herself in Olivia's arms. It was contingent on her getting her father's okay, which was really iffy at the moment, but maybe if she begged.

She walked home shortly before her last period would have let out, feeling weird. It took her a moment to realize the weird feeling was happiness. For the first time since her mom died she felt like *she* wanted to live. She inhaled the air, and it smelled like roses. In New York, the streets never smelled like roses.

Maybe San Francisco wasn't as bad as she originally thought. She thought of Aaron and the way he held her hand and nodded. San Francisco definitely had good things about it.

Smiling, she let herself into the house and went to the kitchen. "Hey, Iliana, I'm home."

Except instead of Iliana, her dad was waiting for her.

She stopped abruptly, her smile fading as she saw the expression on his face. If she thought he was angry the morning after she'd snuck out, it was nothing compared to how he looked now. His arms were crossed and his jaw was tight.

He knew she'd been cutting school.

Of course he did. She hadn't done anything

to keep him from finding out except erasing the automated message the attendance office left on their answering machine. Her therapist in New York would have stated that Rachel wanted her dad to find out.

Her therapist might have been right.

Which meant Rachel was crazy, because no one in their right mind would want to deal with a parent who looked like he was about to explode. She swallowed thickly, wanting to run.

But Nicole would tell her she was stronger than that. Besides, it was all her fault anyway. So she took a deep breath and said, "Before you yell at me, can I just say something?"

He just stared at her.

"I'm sorry." She hunched, feeling the weight of everything on her shoulders, wanting to cry suddenly. But she sucked it up so she could finish. "I know I've been a brat and that you're totally justified in sending me to boarding school, but—"

"How do you know about the boarding school?" he asked, his brow furrowing.

"I accidentally saw it on your tablet." She looked at him imploringly. "The thing is, I know

I deserve being sent away, but maybe we could think out of the box and, um, negotiate a settlement or something."

She thought she saw a flare of humor make his lips twitch, but she must have been wrong because he just gave her that angry stare. "The settlement is going to have to be big. You've really screwed up, Rachel. I can't just let this go."

Sighing, she nodded mournfully. "I know."

"But I'm willing to accept some responsibility, too," he said, taking a seat at the table. "You were right. I haven't really been available, and I should have told you when I started dating Jennifer."

She sat across from him, mirroring his stee-pled hands, figuring this was how people posed when they conducted business. "You know the idea of you dating makes me want to puke, right?"

A ghost of a smile crossed his face. "You really have a way with words, Rach."

He hadn't called her Rach in longer than she could remember. Hearing it gave her hope. "Mom used to say that."

"Your mom thought you were a gifted writer."

"I miss her," she said, lowering her head to

hide the sudden tears in her eyes. When her dad's hand covered hers, a drop escaped.

"I miss her, too, sweetheart," he said softly. "I'll always miss her. But she wouldn't have liked it if we lived in a bubble, sad for all eternity. She'd have kicked our butts."

Rachel smiled a little. "I guess."

"No, she definitely would have." He exhaled. "Like she would have if she found out I was even thinking of sending you away, which wasn't a serious consideration, but you've been on a self-destructive path and I didn't know how else to keep you from messing up the rest of your life."

"You weren't sending me away so you could be with Jennifer?" She managed to say the name without gagging.

He shook his head. "In fact, when I told Jennifer what I was thinking, she yelled at me."

"You talked to her about me?" Rachel asked, not sure if she should be happy or angry.

"You're my world, Rach. Of course I talked about you." He cleared his throat. "I'd like you to meet her. I like her. I don't know where it'll go, but I don't want you to be excluded from my life."

She sighed. "Fine, I'll meet her. But I'm going to tell you if she's a loser."

"Fair enough." Her dad stuck out his hand and they shook on it. Then he got all parental again. "About this boy you snuck out with."

She shook her head. "It's not like that."

He raised his brow.

"Okay, I like him, but that's not what was going on that night." She took a deep breath and went for it. "I wrote a poem for Mom and wanted to give it to Griffin Chase."

"Griffin Chase, the singer?" Her dad frowned.

"Remember how Mom loved his music? I thought it'd be so great if he'd put the poem to music and sang it for Mom, and I found out he was going to be at that club. Aaron just helped me get in."

"You were kissing when I saw you, Rachel."

She nodded, mortified that she was discussing this with her dad. "That was it. The only time. I swear."

"You like him."

She sank further down into her chair. Maybe if she wished hard enough, an earthquake would happen and the floor would collapse and she'd fall through.

Her dad stared at her a long time, in complete silence. Then he shook his head. "I'm not sure I can deal with my daughter dating."

"Try having your dad date," she said under her breath.

He chuckled. Then he began to laugh, rich and deep from his belly.

Rachel hadn't heard him laugh like that since her mom had been alive. It made her smile.

"Okay, let's lay out the bullet points of our truce," he said when he stopped laughing. "One, you can't skip school any more. Two, you're grounded for the next two weeks. Sorry, but I have to lay down the law there."

"But we stay in San Francisco, and after I'm not grounded any longer, I can go out with Aaron sometimes."

Her dad sighed. "You being a teenager is going to kill me."

"He's nice, Dad," she said softly.

"Okay. Okay"—he held his hands out—"I'll deal if you promise not to be a brat to Jennifer."

"Fine." She leaned forward, hands braced on the table. "And I get to work part-time in the lingerie store on Sacramento Street. That's not negotiable either."

"Your grades have to come back up," her dad said, warning in his tone. "And we have to have dinner together, just you and me, once a week."

"Okay."

They shook on it, and then he got up and hugged her. She squeezed him tight, burying her face in his chest.

He kissed her temple. "I love you, Rachel."

"I love you, too, Dad."

"Dinner tonight?" he asked as he let go of her.

"Lobster mac and cheese?"

"You got it." He grinned. "I've got some work to go over. How about seven?"

"Okay." She had a few things to do, too. She ran up to her room and opened her laptop to Facebook. Opening a chat window, she hoped he was online.

He was.

AARON HAWKE: I thought you'd been sent to a work prison in Siberia.

RACHEL ROSENBAUM: Close. Dad was pissed.

AARON HAWKE: I'm sorry you got in trouble.

RACHEL ROSENBAUM: It was my fault, but except for my two-week jail sentence it's all good.

AARON HAWKE: We didn't get your poem to Griffin Chase.

RACHEL ROSENBAUM: I'm working on that, but that's not why I messaged you.

AARON HAWKE: You need help with chem homework?

RACHEL ROSENBAUM: Yes, but only if I can help you with English.

AARON HAWKE: I'll be a gentleman and not point out that was our original deal.

RACHEL ROSENBAUM: I'm rolling my eyes at you.

AARON HAWKE: I know.

RACHEL ROSENBAUM: I'm kind of hoping you'll go to a movie or something with me, too.

She waited, watching the screen for his reply. But when he didn't answer, she prodded him.

RACHEL ROSENBAUM: Well?

AARON HAWKE: I'm checking movie times.

Chapter Twenty-four

$\mathcal{F}$OR THE FIRST time since she'd come to Laurel Heights, Rachel walked into school with her head high. For the first time since her mom died she felt...

Hopeful, she decided, smiling to herself. She hitched her bag on her shoulder and headed to her locker.

"Hey Rach!"

She turned as Lydia skidded to a stop in front of her. Lydia looked the way she always did: full of life with the tiniest bit of mischief on the side. Rachel smiled at her, realizing that she'd actually missed her chem-mate. "What's going on?"

"With me?" Lydia's eyes widened. "I was afraid Madison had abducted you and stuffed you in a Dumpster at the back of the school."

Rachel laughed. "It's not out of the realm."

"She's been on a warpath lately." Lydia shook her head. "Whatever you've done to her, bravo."

"Ladies." Aaron stopped next to them. He flashed Lydia a smile and then looked at Rachel. His smile changed, becoming more private, and he touched her arm. "How are you?"

She may have been grounded, but her dad let her use Facebook still, so she'd been chatting with Aaron pretty much as often as she could. They had a date as soon as her sentence was served. "I'm great," she said softly.

He slid his hand down her arm and took hers. "Good."

The warning bell rang. "I need to stop at my locker," Rachel said. She needed her textbook.

"I have to stop at my locker, too, but I'll walk you guys part way." Aaron engaged Lydia in conversation as they walked through the hall.

Rachel had no idea what they were talking about. All she could think about was his hand and the way he held hers. She'd never held a boy's hand before. It was nice—really nice.

She hoped her palm wouldn't get sweaty.

Aaron stopped at the juncture of the two halls. "I'll leave you here. See you in chem, Lydia." He turned to Rachel, leaned down, and kissed her cheek.

She felt her face burn, conscious of the curious gazes the other students were giving them. But she smiled shyly. "See you in chem," she promised softly.

His smile lifted her heart. He squeezed her hand and strode off.

"Now I know what you did to piss Madison off." Lydia gave her a high-five. "Way to go."

"I didn't do it on purpose."

"No, but the result is just as satisfying."

"You're cold-hearted," Rachel began, "and therefore I believe we should be best friends. Want to come over to my house sometime?"

"Yes, please." Lydia grinned at her. "I've got to get to class. We'll plot later."

Happy, Rachel hurried to her locker.

The _sons_ were still there, closing up their lockers. They stiffened when they saw Rachel.

Whatever. She shrugged and went directly to get her things. Maybe if she ignored them, they'd go away.

But they didn't.

Addison spoke first, for a change. "Look, it's Griffin Chase's BFF."

Madison snorted. "It's mean to taunt the mentally challenged, Adds."

Rachel rolled her eyes. She pulled out the book she needed from her locker and shut it before facing them. "It's not going to work, guys. You're wasting your time."

"Why?" Madison got in her face. "Because you lied? Because you're a loser who's not worth our time?"

She had no idea if Griffin Chase would ever see her poem. Nicole had promised he would, but Rachel understood that the chances of him doing anything with it were nonexistent.

It should have bothered her, but it was hard to be upset. Everything was working out, and regardless of whether Griffin Chase used her poem, it was still a great tribute to her mom. She'd shown it to her dad the other night and he'd actually teared up before he'd caught her in a tight hug and apologized for being a douche these past months. (Her word, not his.)

So she shrugged at the ¬sons and smiled. "If you have nothing better to do than harass me, I feel sorry for you."

While they sputtered with indignation, she turned and rushed to class. Walking through the door as the final bell rang, she eased into her seat.

Rachel pulled out her textbook from her bag. She paused and then also withdrew the blank red notebook.

She ran her hand along the outside. It was the last notebook her mom would ever give her.

Her teacher spent the first ten minutes of class taking attendance and reading announcements. So, taking a deep breath, Rachel opened it and picked up a pen.

Mom, I screwed up. Big time.

But I think I'm done now. I thought that life ended the day you died, and when it kept going on I got pissed. But Dad and Nicole (and everyone really) are right: you'd hate it for us to be unhappy for the rest of our lives.

So when I thought life ended that day, I was wrong. My life began — new and different.

I'm sorry I haven't been writing, but I will. I'll going to start a new story right here, maybe about a girl who has the best mother in the world. Write what you know, right?

Love — always,

Me

Chapter Twenty-five

"You left town and didn't tell me!" KT exclaimed. "What the hell?"

"Come on, you're happy I'm gone." Grif grabbed a bottled water from the refrigerator and walked through his apartment, down the hall to his office. "Admit it. It's better that I'm here moping. Unless you'd rather have me moping in your home."

"I really wouldn't."

"I didn't think so." He smiled faintly, sitting in his desk chair. Since he'd been back, he alternated between self-pity and bouts of non-stop work. Roddy was happy, at least. His manager had loved *Here with You*.

Grif had had a word or two with Roddy about his high-handed publicity tactics. Roddy had acted superior, saying that maybe if Grif had answered his phone, he wouldn't have had to resort to extreme measures. The PR had pleased the studio execs, and Roddy figured Grif should be grateful.

Grateful for coming between him and Nicole? Not that he could really blame his manager. The situation was his doing—his and Nicole's.

"So she kicked you to the curb, huh?" KT said with her usual tact. "I knew it'd happen."

"Tell me why we're friends again?" he asked as he twisted open the water.

"You love me. Be honest, you miss me."

He did, amazingly enough. He missed San Francisco, too. He whirled his chair around and stared out of the floor-to-ceiling windows of his condo. His apartment was spacious and looked out onto L.A., which really wasn't saying much. The skyline was gray from smog, and the apartment itself was amazingly sterile.

Mostly though, he missed Nicole. Everything about her, from the abandoned way she kissed him to the feel of her body snug against his. He even missed how she left her shoes around for him to trip on.

"Hello?" KT boomed into the receiver. "Are you back to moping?"

Sighing, he turned around and opened his laptop. "I miss her, KT."

"Explain to me what happened again. She found out you proposed to that Norwegian string bean and had a fit?"

"You're just as thin as Inga."

"Please don't compare me to her." KT audibly shuddered. "I met her once. You're lucky you escaped her talons. Let's talk about Nicole instead."

"Because you'd like to torture me?"

"Because you need a kick to the butt. Are you really going to let her get away? You obviously like her."

He loved Nicole, but he wasn't going to give KT more ammunition. "She kicked me to the curb, as you so lovingly pointed out."

"Yeah, but all that's just a negotiation, right? Isn't that how relationships work?"

"You're asking me?"

"Well, it's not like I have a great example in my parents."

He clicked on his email, and as he waited for

it to load he started going through the mail piled on the corner of his desk. "Your parents have been together for almost thirty years."

"And they never fight," KT said. "It's unnatural. They're aliens or something."

He stalled on an envelope, recognizing the handwriting even though he hadn't seen it in a long time. He glanced at the return information to be sure. Nicole James. "I have to go, KT," he said slowly.

"I'll play a dirge for your love life." She snickered.

"I'm glad my misery amuses you."

"Sing her a song. Chicks dig pop stars."

"I sing crossover hits," he protested to the dial tone. Shaking his head, he ended the call and opened the letter.

A crinkled, folded piece of paper fell on his lap. He set it on the table and read the note from Nicole.

Grif,

I know you're wondering how I got your address. Your mom gave it to my mom, who gave it to me. You know how that goes.

But I did ask for it. I have a favor to ask. I know this girl who's a big fan of yours. Her mom died and she wrote a poem, and she wants you to set it to music and sing it really badly. Apparently she and her mom used to listen to your music together all the time.

I know it's probably not likely, so I sent it to you hoping maybe you could sign it and send it back to her.

I hope you don't hold our relationship against Rachel's request. She's a great kid— this would mean a lot to her.

Thank you,

N

Unfolding the other sheet of paper, he read the poem. It brought tears to his eyes. He thought about KT's mention of a dirge. This poem was perfect for it. In fact, he could hear the music.

He closed his eyes, leaning back, and tapped out the harmony he heard in his head. Something simple. Something sweet. Pretty much how he felt since he'd lost Nicole.

Chapter Twenty-six

*N*ICOLE LOOKED AT the charts and figures that Valentine had laid out for her, and her only thought was that she thought she might keel over. That was a problem, because Grounds for Thought was especially busy that afternoon and there wasn't much room around them to pass out.

Valentine leaned forward, her face bright with excitement. "What do you think?"

"I think I'm going to throw up." She put her chin on her fist and stared hopelessly at all the information. "I'm not sure I can do this."

"I started my own business," Marley said. "If I can do it, you can, too."

"But you're a talented photographer," Nicole pointed out.

"And you're a talented designer. Seriously,

Nicole"—Marley gestured to the sketchpad that had become Exhibit A—"why have you been hiding this? You draw all the time, but I didn't know you could draw like *that*. Why haven't you done this sooner?"

She shrugged, hugging herself. "I don't know, guys. What if I can't do it? What if I bomb? What if—"

"What if you never try, and you end up working in a little shop for the rest of your life?" Marley said bluntly.

"Not that there's anything wrong with working in a little shop," Valentine said quickly. "But you yourself said you wanted more. This is it."

"What if I'm not ready?" She picked up her teacup and then put it back down. Whoever decided chamomile had soothing qualities lied. "Just the thought of what it's going to take is making me hyperventilate."

Valentine pulled one of the sheets of paper lining the table surface forward. "That's why I broke out everything you need to do in stages. If you tick off each item on this list one at a time, in order, you'll be fine."

Nodding, she looked over the list. There was still time to run. She'd heard Guatemala was nice this time of year. "Maybe I should wait until I'm in a better place in life."

"Nicole, you can't wait, because ducks don't line up." Marley pursed her lips in thought. "Well, actually, they kind of do, which is where the expression came from, but you know what I'm saying."

She shook her head. "No, actually I don't."

Valentine slapped her hand on all the pages she'd compiled and leaned in like an enforcer, which should have been funny considering she looked like a pixie but only made her seem more menacing. "Just do it, Nicole."

Marley smirked. "Or Valentine will kick your butt."

"Okay." She took a deep breath. "Okay, I'll do it."

Valentine smiled happily. "Good."

The door burst open, slamming against the wall. Everyone in the café silenced for a moment as two teenagers rushed in.

Nicole frowned. "Rachel? Is school out for the day?"

"Barely. We ran all the way here to make it

in time." The girl paused to breathe, still holding onto the hand of the boy next to her.

A cute boy. Nicole winked at Rachel.

The teenager blushed. "I know, right? Aaron's *hot*."

"You really do have a way with words," the boy said, looking at Rachel adoringly.

The girl gave him a brilliant smile before facing Nicole. "But that's not why I'm here. He emailed me! Griffin Chase!"

At Grif's name, she froze. Her heart did a series of crazy flops before beating really hard. But she wasn't surprised that he'd emailed the teenager. Griffin was a good man. He wouldn't just leave Rachel dangling, not when it obviously meant so much to her. "What did he say?" she managed.

"He told me to listen to the radio. He's doing an interview." Her eyes widened with disbelief and excitement. "He isn't going to...?"

"There's only one way to find out. When is his interview?"

"*Now*." Rachel bounced with impatience. "He told me to tell you to listen, too. He insisted, actually."

Hope caught in her chest, making it difficult to breathe. "Why would he want me to listen?"

Marley rolled her eyes. "Duh."

"We have to listen," Valentine declared. She looked around. "How do we listen?"

Nicole held her hands up. "The only time I listen to the radio is in my mom's car, when I'm home visiting."

"Eve," Marley exclaimed, jumping up and running to the counter. After a brief discussion with the owner, she yelled, "What station?" across the crowded room.

The room stilled again, which gave Rachel the perfect opportunity to yell the station back. "It's in Los Angeles," she added.

"No worries," Eve called out. "They all broadcast over the Internet. We'll get him on the speakers."

"What's going on?" another patron said in the expectant silence.

"True love," Valentine called back.

The guy at the table next to them nodded. "Can't argue with true love."

Nicole resisted the urge to lean over and give him a smacking kiss on his cheek.

"We're excited today to have Griffin Chase in our studios," a radio DJ enthused suddenly over the café speakers.

"Turn it up," a customer yelled from the back.

A murmur of consensus went through Grounds for Thought. Eve shrugged and cranked it.

"You've joined Captain Kirk, and my special guest, Griffin Chase. Griffin, it's a pleasure to have you here today."

"Thank you, Kirk," Grif said, his voice low and sexy.

But Nicole knew it was sexier in bed, in the middle of the night, when he was holding her and telling her his dreams. It was sexier in the morning, when he woke up and his eyes brightened as he said good morning to her, and it was even sexier when he beat her at Scrabble.

She *missed* him. She clutched her middle, listening avidly.

"Griffin, you're coming out with a new single called *Here with You*," the announcer said. "How would you feel about giving our audience a preview of the song?"

Grif chuckled. "I thought you might ask so I brought Tallulah."

"Tallulah?" the DJ and half of Grounds for Thought asked at once.

"His guitar," Nicole said as Grif answered, "My guitar."

Marley wrinkled her nose. "He named his guitar? Isn't that weird?"

"*Shh.*" Valentine gave her a prim, quelling look.

Over the airwaves, the entire café hushed as he tuned his guitar. He paused and then started singing softly.

With him streaming over the loudspeakers, it felt like he was in the same room with her. Nicole closed her eyes and let him serenade her. When he reached the chorus, he sang from his heart. *"I'm here with you. Kiss me, take me, love me..."*

A hand touched her arm.

Nicole opened her eyes to find Marley's face in hers. "He wrote that for you?" her friend asked incredulously.

She nodded unable to say anything.

The song ended and then Grif said, "This

next one is special. It won't be on this album, but I thought I'd share it today. It's called *A Song for Wendy.*"

Rachel gasped.

Nicole looked up to see joyful tears in the girl's eyes. She took Rachel's free hand and squeezed as Grif began to sing along with the beautiful, haunting music.

You moved away—

a new house

a new life perhaps more blurred than

the one you left behind.

Now you live beneath a roof of grass

screened in by your own name.

If I found your forwarding address could I

contact you?

Could I express my rage that you left without

warning?

If I touched the stone door of your home

would you feel my grief?

The last strains of the song trailed away like wisps of smoke, and the DJ's exuberant voice came back online. "Griffin, that was *amazing.*

We're going to take callers in a second, but first maybe you'll answer a few questions. I've loved all your albums, but your first has always had a special place in my heart, and *Here with You* is reminiscent of it. Was that conscious?"

There was a pause, as though Grif was thinking. Then he said, "Actually, my first album was influenced by a friend. While I was pulling together this new album, also called *Here with You*, I spent some time with her, so it'd be reasonable to say that it'd have the same flavor."

"Is her name by any chance Wendy?" the DJ asked with a verbal leer.

"No, it's not," Grif replied sternly. "*A Song for Wendy* is a tribute to a woman who died before her time. The lyrics were written by Rachel Rosenbaum, her daughter."

"That's me!" Rachel shouted triumphantly.

The café broke out in applause and whistles. The teenager glowed happily, and Nicole squeezed her hand.

"*Here with You*," Grif continued, "was inspired by a dear friend. I've known her most of my life."

"A romantic interest?"

"She's always been my best friend," Grif answered calmly.

Marley threw her hands in the air. "What does that *mean*?"

"You have to find out, Nicole. You *have* to call and ask." Valentine began poking furiously at her phone. Then she held it out to Nicole. "Take it."

"What?" Nicole stared at it, confused. Valentine never gave up her phone. She had a relationship with it that defied reason.

Valentine just shooed her.

"It's not like they'll take my call," she said, letting go of Rachel's hand to take the phone. "Do you know how many people probably call in?"

"Let's take a question from you. Caller One, you're on the radio with Captain Kirk and Griffin Chase," Nicole heard, both over the speakers and in her ear.

What? Her mouth went dry and she gripped the phone.

"Caller One, are you there?"

"Hello?" she said tentatively.

An exclamation went through the entire café.

"Caller One, welcome to Rock Out with Captain Kirk. What's your name, honey?"

"Nicole."

"Nicole, do you have a question for Griffin Chase?" the DJ repeated.

She could hear the eye-roll in his voice, and it was enough to pull her together. "Yes, I do. Grif—*Griffin*, I was wondering about your inspiration for *Here with You*. What's your friend like?"

Without missing a beat, he said, "She's the loveliest person I've ever known, and I wish her all the happiness in the world."

"What if she doesn't want happiness?" she asked. "What if she wants you?"

Valentine smacked a hand on her forehead and shook her head.

"I mean," Nicole amended quickly, "what if *you* make her happy? What if she'd be miserable without you in her life?"

"Then I'd do everything in my power to make her happy for the rest of my life," he said without pause. "She deserves that and more. She deserves to be treasured and respected, and reminded how great and talented she is."

Nicole nodded. "Good to know. Thanks. And your new single is awesome."

She hung up.

The entire café roared in protest.

Nicole stood up and blew a kiss to the crowd and motioned to Eve to turn the radio off. "Thank you for the support, everyone," she said and then sat back down. She put a hand to her chest, afraid her heart was going to jump out.

Rachel was the first to speak. "You adults are crazy."

Yes, she was crazy, but sometimes you had to take a chance. Or two chances, she thought as she looked at the papers spread in front of her.

Nicole didn't hear from Grif all night. No phone call. No text. No email.

She opened Romantic Notions early the next morning, because she needed something to do instead of pacing in her apartment, wondering if he was serious about what he'd said.

Of course he was serious. She shook her head as she rearranged the sketches she'd lined up on the counter for the tenth time. Grif never said something he didn't mean. If he said he wanted to make her happy for the rest of his life, he meant it. When "forever" started was the thing in debate here.

Sighing in disgust—at herself—she focused on the designs. Valentine had found her a manufacturer. Once they found a backer, they could begin production. Finding a backer seemed like an impossible task, but Valentine had assured her it wouldn't take much.

It was overwhelming and scary. She could lose everything.

Except she had nothing to lose. She exhaled and studied her designs. Quickly, she weeded out the ones that didn't fit with the story she had in mind for her first season's line: true love.

The door chimed open.

She started to smile as she looked up, but it died on her lips when she saw who stood in the doorway.

Setting his guitar case next to the door, Grif took his cowboy hat off and crushed it in his hand. "I've been trying to get here since last night. I had a TV interview I was committed to, and it went late so I missed the last flight out. And then this morning my flight was cancelled and the one I was bumped to was delayed."

She swallowed thickly. "Maybe the universe was trying to keep you from coming here."

"No, the universe was testing me to see how badly I wanted this."

"You're here," she said carefully.

"I want this." In his voice, there was more rock-solid certainty than she'd ever heard from him, and that was saying something. He gazed at her steadily.

"I can't change who I am, Nic. This is what you get, so you've got to be sure you want it."

"I do. I want it. I want you."

He didn't make a move, as if he didn't believe her.

She'd make him believe her. She moved to-ward him. "You know how my parents always told me I could be anything and do anything I wanted? That I just had to find my passion?"

He nodded, putting his hands in his pocket.

"I was so scared I'd pick something as my passion and then find out I didn't love it. You were right, I bounced from thing to thing, always second-guessing myself. I was the same with men, because I was never sure any of them were the one I could give myself to forever."

"Forever is—"

"Unreasonable." She shrugged. "I know, but that's what I want. The man I pick is going to be forever, because I believe marriage isn't something you play with."

"Nicole," Grif said quietly, "I've loved you forever, and I'll keep loving you."

She walked up to him and put her arms around him. "Even when I'm old and wrinkly?"

"I can't wait till you're old and wrinkly, because it'll mean I've had that many years to kiss you." He traced her lips. "Your smile will always be mine."

"All of me is yours. *I love you.*" She infused it with as much emotion as she could, knowing that there was no possible way to convey everything she felt for him. Except...

She reached around her neck, pulled the arrowhead over her head, and slipped it over his head. It settled over his heart. "Where it belongs," she said.

"Where you belong," he said, catching her up in his arms and kissing her.

All the longing from the time he'd been gone rose to the surface, an unstoppable tide that had her desperately grappling for more. She touched every part of him, over and under his clothes, and gasped as his hands greedily moved over her, too.

He picked her up by her haunches, and she gripped his waist with her thighs as he whirled them around and headed to the dressing room in the back.

"We can't do it here," she protested. Not that it stopped her from undoing his belt. "I want you in my bed."

Pushing her up against the mirror, he didn't stop kissing her as he spoke. "It was a challenge make it back here much less your bedroom. Next time."

She clawed his back, under his shirt. "As long as next time is soon."

"Have I mentioned that I love your little skirts?" His hand reached under her plaid skirt, pushing it up. "But you weren't very considerate wearing tights."

"A real man would do something about it."

He gripped her tights and ripped them from her. "Like that?"

A thrill of excitement raced through her. "You always know what I need."

"I do." He framed her face with his hand, looking directly in her eyes. "I always will, Nic."

And then he slowly pushed into her.

Her head fell back against the mirror. It was tight and wonderful. "I've missed you," she said again, fervently.

"Thank goodness you came to your senses." He grinned at her and then began to thrust back and forth into her, slow and deliberate, keeping her gaze the entire time.

She dug her heels into his haunches, arching herself into him. "I won't be a groupie."

"I don't want a groupie. I want the sweet, sassy girl I fell in love with when I was twelve."

Her heart melted, and she flung her arms around him. "She's yours."

"Forever," he said, and then he proved it.

Epilogue

One year later...

DIM LIGHTING.

Gauzy curtains.

The fizz of champagne.

The buzz of conversation and laughter.

A deep red runner, sprinkled with white rose petals.

Grounds for Thought was transformed into a romantic bower.

All for her.

Nicole exhaled, trying to blow the huge butterflies out of her belly. This was the day she'd been working feverishly toward for the past year, and now that it was here she just wanted to get it over with.

What if she bombed?

What if the critiques called her a hack?

What if people didn't like her designs?

Valentine headed straight to her, a wrathful pixie dressed like June Cleaver. "Drink this now," she ordered, shoving a glass of champagne into her hand. "And then smile. You look like you're going to be sick."

"It's a distinct possibility."

Her friend got in her face, so that all she could see was Valentine's big blue eyes. "You aren't going to be sick. You're going to shine and make us all proud."

"Okay," Nicole said obediently.

"Good." Valentine smoothed her dress and looked around with a satisfied nod.

A flash caught her attention. Nicole turned.

Marley snapped another photo and then lowered her camera. "This is awesome. I can't believe how this all came together. You'd never guess this is normally a café bookstore. It looks like everyone put their stamp on it."

They had. As Nicole looked around, she felt a surge of love for the community who'd pulled together to support her. Eve had donated the location, and Olivia had insisted on decorating. Julie, from Back to the Fuchsia, arranged all the flowers, making the space vibrant with life. Eve had talked Daniela Rossi, the world-famous pastry chef, to bake special little cakes and truffles. Even Lola Carmichael, a local bestselling romance author, helped by sprinkling fairy dust on the lingerie marketing copy.

The women were all there, too. Eve, Olivia, Lola, and Daniela were chatting with Nicole's mom, all of them drinking champagne—except Olivia, who was just starting to show with her second baby. A tall red-haired woman dressed like a gypsy joined them, and they all laughed.

On the other side of the room, Julie fussed with her flowers last minute, making sure everything was perfect.

And, of course, Marley and Valentine were with her. Nicole linked her arms through theirs. "I love you guys, you know that, right?"

"I'm glad you told us, because I've been having doubts," Marley said with her usual sarcasm. Then she winked and lifted her camera. "I'm going to scope out the best spot for the show. See you."

Valentine shook her head, following Marley with a fond gaze. "Where did we find her?"

"I don't know, but we were lucky."

Her friend patted her back and then pushed her toward the crowd of reporters. "Breathe. And circulate. You're a star tonight."

"Yes." Nicole nodded and stepped forward.

A reporter came over and began to ask questions about Nicole's unprecedented show.

It was unorthodox and risky staging it in a neighborhood café. She'd been told that her first show should be in New York, in the Fall, not Spring in San Francisco. She'd been told that this "plebian" setting would do nothing to launch her line, and that if she went ahead with it, she'd be relegated to the small time.

But Nicole started in Laurel Heights. Without the women who'd befriended her, she'd still be jumping from job-to-job, unsure of what she really wanted. This lingerie show was to launch her line, but it was also an homage to the community and the women who'd supported her.

Fortunately, her investor had backed her decision. But Prescott Carrington-Wright III was a god-among-men. Nicole didn't know why Scott had decided to invest in her start-up, but she was grateful for him every day.

Scott had assured her the instinct to set the first show in Laurel Heights was a good one. He'd hired a marketing guru to help spin the event, and the media had picked up on it. They called it "innovative," "fresh," and "the power of community"— pretty much everything their marketing consultant had told them it'd be. All the big guns were there tonight: *Vogue*, *W*, *InStyle*, and *Cosmo*, to name a few.

"I'm going to borrow Nicole for a moment," a deep voice said from behind.

She turned to see Scott. He looked like he always did—powerful and in control. She bet he intimidated most people, but she'd liked him immediately. "Did you come to rescue me?"

"No way." He smiled. "You looked in your element. This is all fabulous and completely beyond what I'd imagined. They're in for a treat tonight."

"It's pretty great, isn't it?" She beamed.

"Better than great." He paused, and then said, "Who's that woman over there?"

She looked to where he pointed. "Julie? She did the flowers."

He nodded, his gaze completely focused on the woman.

Nicole frowned. "Is anything wrong?"

"Not at all." He squeezed her arm. "Excuse me."

She watched him walk over to the florist. Like a deer scenting danger, Julie looked up as he approached, her body language stiff.

Was something wrong? Nicole started to join them, but then she saw Scott's smile, predatory, his focus completely on Julie. *Ah.* So it was like *that*.

"What are you grinning about?" Grif said softly, coming up behind her and kissing her neck.

She hugged the arm that he slipped around her waist. "My money man is making moves on the florist."

"Good for him." Grif nuzzled her temple. "Maybe he'll get lucky, like us."

She turned into his arms. "No one is as lucky as us."

The lights dimmed, signaling the start of the show.

Grif kissed her softly. "Go be a star."

"Okay." She felt the familiar flutter of nerves but excitement overrode it. She went and accepted the microphone from the sound technician and faced everyone. "Thank you all for joining me tonight for the launch of *Romance, by Nicole*."

She nodded at the sound guy, who kicked off the music: Grif's latest album, *Here with You*, which had gone platinum in the first week of its release.

She held her breath as the first "model" walked out from the back. In keeping with the community theme, Nicole had wanted to use customers from Romantic Notions to show off the designs — everyday women of all sizes and shapes, transformed into passionate dreams.

The next model came out: Rachel.

Nicole smiled. Talk about transforming — the girl had done just that in the past year. She was lovely, and in the modest babydoll she looked both adorable and stunning. Her boyfriend Aaron certainly thought so, if his cheering was any indication.

The teenager winked at Nicole and then strutted down the red carpet.

Nicole watched model after model parade through the room, showing off her creations, and felt so blessed. She clasped her hands to her chest and tried to keep it in.

"Who's that?" Bull asked softly, coming up alongside her.

She glanced at the woman on the red carpet that his gaze was trained on. "Joey? She lives in the neighborhood. She shops at Romantic Notions."

He growled low and deep in his throat, like he was hungry. If the way he was looking at Joey was any indication, he was hungry for her. "She looks like my size."

Nicole remembered the red lingerie he'd bought and looked at him, impressed. "She is, actually."

"I could tell."

Smiling, Nicole patted his arm. "She'll be around after the show."

"I'm gonna make sure of it." He kissed her cheek and disappeared into the crowd.

When the last model strode out wearing white bridal lingerie, the entire room burst into applause.

Grif handed her flowers, careful to stay out of her limelight. "It was perfect, Nic," he said, giving her a proud kiss. "Just like you."

"No." Nicole laughed happily, throwing her arms around him, aware of the flash of cameras going off and not caring. "It was perfect like us, just like it should be."

Don't miss the rest of the Laurel Heights series!

Also fall in love with Kate Perry's sexful, playful novels of family and love including *Playing Doctor* and *Playing for Keeps*...

Playing Doctor

After catching her research partner-slash-fiancé with the intern, Dr. Daphne Donovan returns home to lick her wounds and figure out how to fix her life. It doesn't take a genius to figure it out: being an uber-brilliant Doogie Howser has made her life miserable while all the normal people she knows are happy and content.

There's only one thing to do: become normal. No more being the wunderkind of childhood disease research. All she wants is a regular nine to five job, two-point-five children, a white picket fence, and a blue collar husband.

Except normal isn't all it's cracked up to be, especially after she meets Ulysses Gray. Gray is everything she doesn't want: smart, incredibly handsome, and a doctor--just like her ex-fiancé. She wants to deny him--and herself--but she can't resist playing doctor...

Playing for Keeps

Since her mother's death more than fifteen years before, Grace Connors has been the matriarch of her family. She's put her own dreams on hold to raise her younger sisters and keep her ex-marine father in line.

So when her sister Nell decides to get married, it's on Grace to make it a wedding their mother would have been proud of. It can't be hard to organize a party, right?

But then everything falls apart, including her budding romance with her sexy best friend Pete. Caught in the crossfire with the enemy at her back, will Grace be able to fix it all before she becomes a casualty of love?

Legend of Kate

Kate has tangoed at midnight with a man in blue furry chaps, dueled with flaming swords in the desert, and strutted on bar tops across the world and back. She's been kissed under the Eiffel Tower, had her butt pinched in Florence, and been serenaded in New Orleans. But she found Happy Ever After in San Francisco with her Magic Man.

Kate's the bestselling author of the Laurel Heights novels, as well as the Family and Love and Guardians of Destiny series. She's been translated into several languages and is quite proud to say she's big in Slovenia. All her books are about strong, independent women who just want love.

Most days, you can find Kate in her favorite café, working on her latest novel. Sometimes she's wearing a tutu. She may or may not have a jeweled dagger strapped to her thigh…

Made in the USA
Lexington, KY
28 January 2014